Praise for *How I Became a*

Finalist for the Center for Fictio

"From the shocking opening of her debut novel . . . Krys Lee invites us into a world Westerners rarely glimpse and can barely imagine. . . . While tackling weighty themes of power and politics, Lee zooms in laserlike on minute details to create moments of startling intimacy. . . . Despite the violence it encompasses, at the heart of the story is a belief in the human capacity to transcend hardship, and to hope."
—*O, The Oprah Magazine*

"A compelling vision of both North and South Korea."
—Alexander Chee, *The New York Times Book Review*

"An intense, unforgettable, compassionate study of human resilience . . . What Lee teaches us is that there is hope in the most desperate of circumstances, that the human spirit can still sputter to life after the worst has happened."
—*The Miami Herald*

"The plot is full of drama and the writing is crystal clear . . . The more confusing and horrible our world becomes, the more critical the role of fiction in communicating both the facts and the meaning of other people's lives. Krys Lee joins writers like Anthony Marra, Khaled Hosseini, and Elnathan John in this urgent work."
—*San Francisco Chronicle*

"[Lee] eloquently draws attention to issues of displacement, loss, and identity, and to China's record of human rights abuses against North Korean refugees."
—*The New York Times*

"A novel of great sincerity and moral courage, a book that can stand as a resonant response to the challenge that fiction has no place in the white heat of political turmoil."
—*Financial Times*

"[An] elegant, devastating novel."
—*Minneapolis Star-Tribune*

"Lee's story throws light on a place we know little about, in heart-wrenching, lyrical detail."   —*Elle*

"Krys Lee is a superb writer. . . . Lee has worked with North Korean refugees and she knows intimately their terror when trying to survive in a world where it is impossible to distinguish between friend and foe."
—Barbara Demick, *The Guardian* (London)

"A masterful portrayal of the personal side of world politics."
—*BookPage*

"Lee successfully creates well-formed characters and makes readers care about their struggles. . . . [It's] impossible to read this novel without remembering . . . that many real-life refugees have faced similar tough decisions and horrors in order to escape."
—*The Christian Science Monitor*

"A powerful tale."   —*Ladies' Home Journal*

"An ode to friendship. And freedom."   —*New York Post*

"Krys Lee takes readers past the border and deep into the lives of defectors. . . . *How I Became North Korean* is both delicate and menacing; the book's details are fascinating, along with its social and political background. However, it is, most of all, an overwhelming, emotional story. Lee's book is shaped by its characters' fragility, but mostly driven by their courage."   —*The Millions*

"An extraordinary narrative that is both contemporary testimony and literary achievement . . . [Krys Lee is] one of the most elegant, impeccable voices of her youthful generation. Devotees of authors able to navigate effortlessly between short and longer forms, including Jhumpa Lahiri and Adam Johnson, will certainly be blessed to discover Lee's work."   —*Library Journal* (starred review)

"Haunting . . . A vivid and harrowing read."   —*Publishers Weekly*

Krys Lee is the author of the short-story collection *Drifting House*, which won the Story Prize Spotlight Award and was named an honor title in adult fiction by the Asian/Pacific American Librarians Association. A recipient of the Rome Prize and a finalist for the BBC International Short Story Award, she has published fiction, journalism, and literary translations in *Granta*, *The Kenyon Review*, *Narrative*, the *San Francisco Chronicle*, *Corriere della Serra*, and *The Guardian*, among others. She is an assistant professor of creative writing and literature at the Underwood International College of Yonsei University in South Korea.

www.kryslee.com

How I
Became a
North Korean

Krys Lee

PENGUIN BOOKS

PENGUIN BOOKS
An imprint of Penguin Random House LLC
375 Hudson Street
New York, New York 10014
penguin.com

First published in the United States of America by Viking Penguin,
an imprint of Penguin Random House LLC, 2016
Published in Penguin Books 2017

ISBN 9780670025688 (hardcover)
ISBN 9780143110507 (paperback)
ISBN 9780735221307 (international edition)
ISBN 9780399563935 (e-book)

Printed in the United States of America
10 9 8 7 6 5 4 3 2 1

Set in Granjon
Designed by Nancy Resnick

This is a work of fiction. Names, characters, places, and incidents either are the product of the
author's imagination or are used fictitiously, and any resemblance to actual persons, living or dead,
businesses, companies, events, or locales is entirely coincidental.

To those who have crossed

The question for me was always whether that shape we see in our lives was there from the beginning or whether these random events are only called a pattern after the fact. Because otherwise we are nothing.

—Cormac McCarthy, *All the Pretty Horses*

Contents

Part I

Crossing

Yongju

Home still begins as an image for me. The Pyongyang subway line dug down as deeply as a bunker. The elderly drunk and dancing by the Pothong River to the brass *kwaengwari*'s tinsel music. The electric fences circling hundreds of labor camps farther north that we pretended didn't exist. These images are my home, my prison sentence. But memory is a slippery mirror, a surface that splinters into fragments when I touch it. It moves the way that the poems I used to write changed with each attempt at completion; it haunts me. I find myself looking for clues to the past, repeatedly returning to that mansion floating in light, to our country that the rest of the world calls North Korea.

I'm haunted by what my *eomeoni* told me. On that last night, she said, no one wanted to be present in the mansion with kilometers of bomb shelter tunnels underneath it. She and my *abeoji* wore the same smiles as everyone else, the same fur coats and Rolex watches engraved with the name of the Dear Leader, the

Great General, the man with dozens of honorific titles. They wore the same Kim family badges over their hearts and, in this way, demonstrated their loyalty to our leaders.

We, the children, were absent. But our parents entered the spacious hall set up for a banquet, saying to one another, "I hear your son will attend Kim Chaek University—you must be so proud of him!" or "I saw your daughter play the cello—what a beauty she is!"

We were safe topics. They knew one another from the same schools, the same committees. Their sons, like me, were exempt from the ten years of required military service and grew up in Pyongyang's top institutions, and their daughters, like my little *dongsaeng,* were expected to someday marry their equals. Our *eomeoni* in silk dresses and hair coiled into buns sat at one side of a long mahogany table, our *abeoji* in black suits on the other. They looked as if they were enjoying themselves, but everyone was afraid. It could have been any party except for those badges and our Dear Leader at the foot of the table, observing them all.

This was my family's Pyongyang in 2009. We didn't know anyone who was exiled to grim mining towns or ground tree bark into their stews in order to fill their stomachs. We shared nothing in common but citizenship with the schoolkids living in the provinces forced to do work in opium fields, or the communities of men roving the country looking for work to seek money that became food. As for me, I lived the life that my *abeoji*'s and *eomeoni*'s status allowed me; I read and spoke passable English, Russian, and a little Chinese, and expected to attend graduate school overseas. I was twenty-one and assumed my journey would be easy.

In that hall my *eomeoni* and *abeoji* must have seemed untouchable as they glided under a chandelier as heavy as a tank. It hurts to conjure up the image of my *eomeoni,* her face the innocent shape of an egg, her hazel eyes gazing ahead frankly, though she trusted no one. She, a well-known actress, weaved toward my *abeoji*'s lover with fluid movements, a walk she had constructed through hundreds of hours of practice. After greeting those she passed, she sat across from a woman with false eyelashes, and, in a tone she reserved for children, said, "You got home rather late last Friday evening, didn't you?"

In this way, she reminded the woman that there was only one wife and that the wife had generously permitted the husband a tryst with his lover. My *eomeoni*'s fierce pride disguised her wounds like a cloak.

My *abeoji* was a man confident that his decisions were right. He wasn't too alarmed, and smiled jauntily as he sat beside my *eomeoni.* He ran the government trading bureau, a powerful position mysterious even to his family; there were always graver issues for him than women. But as his lover flushed and leaned like a sunflower toward her unknowing husband, my *abeoji* whispered to my *eomeoni,* "Was this necessary?"

She said, "Does it matter?"

She tilted her chin high, lifting her neckline to hide the subtle physical changes incurred over their marriage arranged by the Great General himself. My *abeoji* didn't notice, or care, about such details. But she cared about her unsmudged red lipstick, about protecting her dignity. That last night she upheld her part perfectly until there was no part left to uphold.

To the wife of the number eleven rank in the party who was next to her, she said, "How was your *eomeoneem*'s surgery?" then "How was the honey I sent over?" Surrounded by the group of forty guests, fenced in by their limited freedoms, my pragmatic *eomeoni* maintained her alliances. Minutes later she said to the number seven man in the party across from her, "The plans in your speech last week will serve our country so well."

As the man blushed and pontificated on trade techniques, my *eomeoni*'s chopsticks hovered over slivers of blowfish and tuna still quivering on the plate, part of the latest shipment from the Tokyo Tsukiji fish market flown in on a private jet. My *abeoji* anticipated the brandy that would be served later; it made him nostalgic for his work trips to Europe, a continent, he had told me, where the whole world was for sale. This was our life.

Before the ruins of the overflowing table and the movable fountain of Chivas Regal were cleared by a dozen attendants, my *eomeoni*'s foot nudged my *abeoji*'s, her eyes insisting on the glass in front of him. He raised his brandy to the Dear Leader's health as prompted and said, "To our Great General!"

Finally they dared to look at him.

The Dear Leader lifted a glass to himself, and only then did all the other glasses in the hall rise in succession. "To our Great General!" the bright, anxious mouths said.

Underneath his gray silk Mao suit, maybe the general suffered, too. I wonder if he touched a discolored mole that worried him, or touched his thinning hair teased into a tangle of height when he was weighing his potential successors, checking if he was still intact. But he knew what to rely on when nothing else was left: extravagant rituals of the hand, goose-stepping parades of soldiers, a skyline of monuments. He sank into the chair that hugged his girth, and with one ragged rhythm of his arm held everyone's attention.

I want the scene to freeze here. I want to prevent the events that my *eomeoni* told me about on the night we left Pyongyang forever; I want my language of yearning to be more powerful than time, but all I can do is remember. Imagine. Believe the only story I have left of my *abeoji*.

In the hall so large that their voices echoed, the Dear Leader's hand rose toward the northernmost wall from him and the wall parted.

The attendants dragged back the red curtains and revealed a stage behind the wall. A glittering disco globe came down from the ceiling and the Joy Brigade began strutting in pink hot pants to a banned American pop song. Everything about the performance, in theory, was banned. The women were too close to the Dear Leader; many would have bleak futures. I would hear about a girl who disappeared to the camps after resisting the Dear Leader's advances; another, who had idealized a visiting Swiss diplomat and lived with her nostalgia; still another who married a stranger because the Dear Leader commanded the match.

The Dear Leader stood up, and everyone averted their eyes. He said sharply, "Why aren't you dancing?" His mood turned from the moment before.

The Dear Leader's words worked; they always worked. The

lights dimmed and strobe lights flashed, and my parents began dancing in the hall that could have been in Paris or Pyongyang.

I don't know how many crimes my *abeoji* committed, or what he did on his business trips setting up trading deals in China and beyond. I don't know who my *abeoji*'s lovers were, or my *eomeoni*'s real birth date. I don't know if they ever tasted wild blackberries. I don't know why my *abeoji* so hungered for power and money, if he was ever deeply lonely. Or why it has taken so many years for me to be able to speak about them. This I do know: Their affection was fierce; battle was the way they demonstrated their love for each other. They were also gentle to each other; they were kind. Still, maybe her hand finally sought him and landed lightly across the outer bone of his hip, quieting his agitation.

She said, "Calm yourself, my love. People are watching."

He murmured, "We will always be together." Always confident.

It was only nine, but soon enough it would be midnight. Shadows stretched as long as train tracks across the walls; the disco ball flickered in and out. They danced, sidestepping across the parquet. At least, those who hadn't disappeared last year. Names that no one spoke in public because they had been banished, imprisoned, or killed. Or maybe, just maybe, escaped. These people I had grown up with were individuals, and they were the same, for they wanted to summit from official party number twenty-four to sixteen; they wanted the Dear Leader's approval; they wanted to be safer. The dancing continued until those around my *eomeoni* began to drag along to the music. But she never allowed herself to drag.

My *eomeoni* only became more correct, resembling more with each hour the actress who looked as if she couldn't possibly have bowel movements like the rest of us. She watched the clock. Midnight. Not long before we were to flee our country. The more the Dear Leader observed them, the more skittish my parents became. Must flatter, must be safe, must not let my face betray, must enjoy myself. I don't want to see it, it's all I can see: my *eomeoni,* in the end, a weak woman, and my *abeoji,* weaker still. The regime that would go on.

Finally, the Dear Leader's hands clamped down on their shoulders, one on my *abeoji*'s, one on hers. "My turn!" he said.

A dance, then what next? Other entanglements, the violation of a marriage? It had happened before. The Dear Leader had no right! My *abeoji*'s narrow lips would have turned south. We learned to hide our thoughts behind well-trained faces, but he was unable to hide his even in front of our leader. Maybe that was the tipping point to the Dear Leader's mood. Our fickle leader, our Great General, he owned every right.

My *abeoji* stepped back, finally retreating. The Dear Leader was drunk, now angry, and made his decision. He reached as if brushing off lint from my *abeoji*'s suit lapel, then motioned a bodyguard over and casually withdrew a revolver from the man's jacket pocket. He aimed it at my *abeoji*'s heart.

All I can do is watch.

The bullet spun out from the barrel, its lead body spiraled and chipped through the breastbone, punctured the pericardial cavity, the diaphragm, then penetrated the left atrium of my *abeoji*'s heart. His hands fluttered as if releasing a dove into the air, a delicate, useless protest as the bullet carved a path through him. He fell forward, his muscles twitching. My *eomeoni*'s hands covered her eyes, and the other people fled to the far corners of the hall. The gun disappeared back into the bodyguard's suit.

The Dear Leader said, "No one steals from me!" He had made an example of my *abeoji*.

Dark liquid seeped from him, his scalp dampened against my *eomeoni*'s hands that were now in his hair. "Won't someone help?" she cried as the great muscle of his heart leaked blood. Blood filled his white shirt, spread to the collar, stained her nails, and infused her hands with the smell of bitter wormwood. In that towering city of my childhood, a traitor, a husband, a father, was there, still there for her, beating, beating, then gone.

2

Danny

One thing I know for sure: 2009 was the start of irreversible changes in my life. That Friday in early March, I opened my locker and discovered my very first love letter. I was sixteen, and church and the Boy Scouts had been the composite of my social life since my family had emigrated from the Autonomous Korean Prefecture in China when I was nine years old. Nothing like this had happened to me before. As I opened the envelope and skimmed the note doused in cologne, my heart went pitter-patter and my palms became slick with sweat. It was unsigned, but I knew the handwriting. It was from Adam Thomas, my physics lab partner. A guy with the long-limbed quickness of a deer and an unruly smile to match his wavy hair.

I'd never had my feelings reciprocated before; or rather, I'd never shared my feelings so that they could be reciprocated. It was a secret I could barely admit to myself. But I trusted that the note asking to meet me was sincere. I'd shot up six inches in the last year and I was confident of my worth, though only a few seemed

11

to recognize it—namely, my mom and dad. Adam and I had been partners the entire semester without once being separated, a pairing that in fact he'd insisted on. Maybe this is the most important thing about faith: I believed because I wanted to believe.

I was the kind of kid who usually spent weekends pestering my youth pastor with earnest questions, occasionally singing hymns in downtown Redlands with our youth group while brandishing a "God Is Salvation" placard, or reading fat tomes and pretending that school dances were beneath my intellectual interests. But that evening I tried to tame my curly hair that exploded like firecracker sparks from my head and camouflage myself in the ugly jeans and overpriced sweatshirt that my peers approved of.

I was so nervous I entertained not showing up that night, but I did finally drive to the hill where the lawyers' and doctors' kids lived. Streetlights and McMansions surrounded the park without a scrap of trash or a wink of graffiti in sight. It was as if the town's entire sanitation force was dedicated to these hills. Even their palm trees smelled like money. None of it made me bitter. I knew that it was easier for a camel to go through the eye of a needle than for a rich man to enter heaven.

I got out of the car and waited with my right profile—my best side—facing outward. My anxiety doubled as it became ten, fifteen minutes past eight, but I tried to be accommodating even if I wasn't exactly an easygoing person. I could learn. I was anxious and hopeful for the first time in months and feeling mostly luminous. I debated whether he might be amenable to attending church. I began wondering if it was just one more joke on me and I should go home.

They came quietly across the grass, and by the time I heard the crunch of gravel, it was too late. I tried to squeeze back into the car, but two guys all bluff and brawn twisted my hands behind me before I was halfway in. As they dragged me away into the dark, I saw that there were four of them in total. The ringleader was Adam.

When I reached out for him, he shoved his hands into his jeans pockets. "Thanks to you, I flunked the midterm. I'll owe my physics grade to you. It was a stupid move, turning me in."

"I didn't turn you in!"

When I'd seen a note float between students during the midterm exam, I had merely behaved responsibly and informed our teacher Mr. Hood.

"It was *you*? I didn't know it was your note."

One of his friends said, "What a fag!"

"You shouldn't be turning anyone in." Adam flung an arm over my shoulders with the kind of confidence that comes from living on the hill all your life. With an ease that felt like a foreign country to me. "What have I ever done to you?"

"I'm sorry, really." I shrank back. And I was sorry I seemed incapable of keeping a low profile like I needed to, sorry I had been dragged to America and away from my known world, sorry to have trusted a guy who didn't deserve my trust. "I'll find ways to repay you. I'm Christian—I keep my promises."

"The whole shitty town knows you're a fanatic. Hard not to, when you stand on street corners screeching God's name." He grabbed a hockey stick and with it poked me in the crack of my butt. "My dad expects Princeton, at worst. You have any idea what you've done?"

He pushed the stick upward, nearly lifting me off the ground. "Get the recorder running," he said. "Insurance he'll keep quiet."

They forced me to strip off all my clothes and hump the hockey stick, fondle myself in front of them, and worse, until they became bored and left for a party.

On Monday I got as far as ten yards from the school's chain-link fence. Those ten yards might as well have been the Pacific Ocean. A sea of students milled in front of me, all potential enemies and not a single ally in sight. I was sure that everyone knew what had happened to me. Gauzy-skirted Anna Hunter passed me, everyone's object of lust who didn't know I existed; then came cliques that treated the prom—a night on which girls across the nation wiped out their savings to resemble a cream puff—as if it were a national security issue. Somewhere, there was Adam. Harvard didn't matter anymore, my parents' hopes didn't matter, nor did a future banking job that would reward me with a handsome vacation home in Hawaii for preying on global markets. Confined in that small space of high school, no camouflage would ever be thick enough for me. I didn't belong there.

For nearly a month I left the house every day and made as if I were going to school. I told myself I was coming up with a plan B, some grand scheme concerning my life, but what I actually did was run away from myself. I skimmed through science journals and comic books in the local library and took long bus rides to the beach and stared out at the brutal ocean, falling back on familiar fantasies about the remarkable life I would have surely led if I hadn't left China. That is, until the day the school contacted my dad.

My dad's complexion went from peach to pomegranate after we left the principal's office, but he didn't say anything in the car. He merely stroked the pocket watch in his palm, one he always kept with him as if it were a beloved aging pet. He was a clockstore manager and the ticktocking surrounding him seemed to satisfy his need for conversation. He took great pride in his job—he called it a "vocation"—and often told strangers that he had once repaired a 1902 Audemars Piguet.

There was no order or reason to the way he drove. We were up in the San Bernardino Mountains one moment, then bordering Fresno the next before backtracking. The gas tank dwindled. Waste was my dad's way of letting me know he was angry.

"You know what happens to people who let go of their routines?" he said, as if I weren't a believer of routines myself. "They end up sucked into the chaos around them. You and I, we're not so good at blending in. But an I.Q. of 150 is your way out. It's a gift from God, if you want to think of it that way."

I managed to stay quiet for once. There wasn't an honest word I could share with him.

When he finally did look at me, he was angrier than I'd ever seen him. He was a good dad. He never hit me or raised his voice. He had also probably never broken a rule in his life. "What you did was wrong. Your only job is to go to school. We don't ask much of you."

I felt, suddenly, very tired. "Abba," I said. "You know sailors used to study maps studded with dragons, mermaids, and sirens, and pray not to fall off the edge of the world. I think I understand how they felt. Did you ever consider there might be a reason I don't want to go to school?"

"Who wants to eat medicine or raise children? You do it because it's the right thing to do—it's good for you." He pulled up in front of our house. "I'm sure you had your reasons, and they were probably very good reasons. But—"

"I know. There are two kinds of people in this world: people with excuses and people without," I said. "You've been saying that since I was in the cradle."

"We never had a cradle."

"Not everything is literal."

He said uncomfortably, "We can fix the problem together."

But there was nothing I could tell him. I agreed to attend school on Monday if he insisted, which sent him into platitudes about the importance of education. The conversation went predictably downhill from there. I didn't know if it was us or our culture or both, but we were always speaking from two different shores, unable to hear each other.

My mom always insisted that my dad and I were exactly alike, but I didn't think we had much in common. One meeting point I was willing to concede was our fondness for habits. I relied on habits to rein me in. I prayed first thing in the morning, then studied five new English vocabulary words before getting out of bed. A breakfast of orange juice and some form of protein always followed. To structure the week, I did a sudoku puzzle daily and read a book every three days. Once a week, I maintained my beloved collection of survival gadgets that my parents augmented each birthday.

The routine that gave my life its most definite shape was being a Christian. Thanks to my mom, I'd been baptized before I could call my parents Eomma and Abba. Compared with my immediate environment, the Bible felt like a known world.

My dad was visibly relieved when he shipped me off that Friday to Big Bear Lake for one of the many church retreats that dotted my yearly calendar. He hadn't known what to do with me since Mom took off for China a few months ago for her first-ever missionary effort, and my skipping school had only made it worse.

But camp was like a shirt buttoned wrong from the start. By the time I arrived I had developed a pimple the size of a wart on my nose. Then the counselors, some of whom I knew from other church retreats in other locations, served us dry pancakes for dinner due to a catering catastrophe. The downhill of my day escalated when I delivered a humiliating, full-throttle solo of "A Mighty Fortress Is Our God," after everyone else stopped singing following the first verse, and, despite the counselors' machinations, was picked second-to-last for Bible Jeopardy, a game everyone should have known I excelled at.

I'd never acquired the mysterious talent for making friends, but that weekend my usual thick skin felt flayed and raw, and without Tobias Lee, my Christian fellow-in-arms who usually kept me company on retreats, the cafeteria felt dreadfully vast. There, despite all our brother, brother, and sister, sister to one another a few hours before, the tired social order asserted itself. The usual predictable groups sat at long tables, from kids with haloes hovering over their heads to kids wearing motorcycle jackets and hiding stashes of pot. Even one of the P.K.s (also known as pastors' kids) was a dealer. There were the cool Christians in preppy shirts and dresses at a table far from the others and a gaggle of colorless personalities crowded grumpily next to them, laughing each time the "cool" ones cracked a joke. It might as well have been a school lunchroom. Some of the nicer ones waved at me when they passed, but I knew I wasn't their first choice or their second or even their seventh. I slid onto a wood bench and sat alone.

I was relieved when Grace Lee came up to my table with a small group behind her. She had a sleek skein of hair and an expression as cheerful as a roll of Life Savers. I'd been in awe of her for all seven years of my life in America, and though she was perennially nice to everyone, including me, her sentences directed at me invariably began with "You're so funny" and was said in a way that suggested "You're so strange."

I pulled together my splayed-out, gangly limbs and sat up straight, trying to appear as normal as I could.

She studied me. "That's the first Noah's ark T-shirt I've ever seen."

"You can get them silk-screen-printed by mail order, if you sketch it first." I spread the shirt out wide so she could see it better. "Isn't it great? It's got all my favorite animals on it."

My elbow knocked into my tray, but a guy with lopsided biceps caught it before it fell.

"Hey, chill out there." He gave me a friendly pat while frantically scanning the room.

What can only be called an awkward silence descended. I had a knack for creating them.

"Plenty of seats." I patted the spot beside me.

"I promised Kate," Grace said apologetically, and I saw her friend waving her over to the end table. "You want to join?"

I knew I wasn't wanted, but I picked up my tray and joined them. That was me, a nutty brown-skinned, elephant-eared guy with God and a collection of finger puppets as companions. A guy more at ease with objects than people. As the others swapped stories and strained to be likable to one another, I spooned up some of the rubbery lasagna. I reminded myself that God was with me and that I was never alone, but I felt like Robinson Crusoe on a deserted island surrounded by bright, chirping parrots.

There were certain myths that I lived by. One of them was that I was fearless. I believed I wasn't afraid of pain or being socially ostracized—that is, until we walked down to the lake the next day. To someone who can't swim, Big Bear Lake might as well have been the Pacific Ocean.

I didn't even like bathtubs, maybe because my father's idea of teaching me to swim was to toss me into the local pool when I was five years old and watch me promptly sink to the bottom. I excelled at all the other survival skills I'd picked up from years of Boy Scouts, but despite a whale's weight of effort I could only paddle for about two minutes before sputtering downward.

The ground on the way to the lake was as hard as an over-baked brownie and crackly with pine needles. I walked behind everyone else, wishing I was heading in the opposite direction, deep into the mountains, past deer tracks and dried-up creek beds, to retreat like Moses and become renewed. I craved the courage to walk away from my life, from Monday, when I would have to face Adam and his friends and find a new map to live by. At the very least, I wanted to return to China, where my life had made more sense to me. As we approached the water, I listened for the omnipresence of God in the dim roar of the motorboats and the water lapping at the lake's shore. I almost heard it.

A blond kayaking instructor straight out of a Scandinavian magazine dumped a set of life jackets near my feet, as if he somehow knew that I needed one the most. The others, who had stepped straight out of a J. Crew catalog in their polo shirts and shorts, talked nonstop to one another without receiving strange looks or offending anyone. These people born with a social finesse I lacked started partnering up, grabbing paddles, and helping each other with their life jackets.

"Okay, kids!" said one of the older youth leaders with a tug to his ginger-colored mustache. He extended his large hands out to each side like race car flags. "Don't be stupid out there—God's always watching."

There were already people rowing out into the lake's endless silver gray, bobbing up and down with each slap of water, no bigger than twigs. The kids ahead of me waded in and pushed off in double kayaks until it was my turn. My hands felt as thick as winter gloves. Finally my single kayak's plastic belly scraped against the sandy bottom and I floated away from the shore.

The other kayaks paddled ahead. I watched a blue heron dip low, thrust its needlepoint beak into the green water, and burst back up with a tiny fish. My fear magnified everything on the lake. A bird's shadow was the size of a baseball field, the murmuring water around me resembled the voices of people. Entire civilizations seemed to be speaking, but not to me. There was a disturbed motion from deep down in the water, and I thought of the Loch Ness monster, of Grendel's lair. I felt a desperate hope that the bright cerulean sky would split apart like a badly stitched bedspread as the Lord and his procession of trumpeting angels marched through, with Michael the archangel in the lead, making his stunning entry. They would clarify my life.

I was leaning over when a motorboat zipped by, the kayak's bow jumped, and I was pitched out. Water plunged up my nose and into my mouth and lungs. I flapped my arms and clung to the straps of the life vest.

"Isn't that Danny?" said some faraway voice. "What's he doing this time?"

Air bubbles rose in front of my stinging eyes. The sun became a distant spot. My arms flailed for the paddle, but it was already floating away. I descended into the dark. All sound was sucked down deep into the lake, and I was seized with the certainty that someone was waiting for me. It became silent.

Only then I blinked, astonished to find myself conscious again. Fish were investigating my dream legs, my dream body that had landed in their watery garden. I bounced in slow motion across a bedrock littered with broken glass and cigarette butts. I vaulted across a path—if a moving mass of dead and living matter can be called a path. I wondered if this was the path to heaven, and I leaped buoyantly from a bed of waterweed that was kissing the bottoms of my feet.

My delusions grew. The algae gave way to a podium and a man behind it barely visible in the murkiness. Someone was waiting. The plants hushed, the fish arced away. The shadow closed in on me. Tiny pieces of coral scraped against the soles of my feet. I was fearful, ecstatic, and reached for the hand of salvation, but suddenly there was no shadow, no water, no peace. Only rough human hands came pumping down on my chest and a mouth over my mouth, in a long, unwelcome kiss.

3

Jangmi

In late February or early March, I walked across the frozen Tumen River toward a man from China, ready to give my unborn child a different life. Of course my crossing had actually started much earlier, maybe with the Great Hunger or even before I was born. The China beyond the river that day was as dried up and brown as my country. I walked with the eyes of men and women following me from both sides of the shore. I remember being hopeful though the riverbanks were still hoary with the remaining snow.

A border patrol who the man from China had bribed followed me across. There were broad, dark patches where the ice looked as thin as glass, but I was from a border town. I had smuggled goods in and out since I was fourteen and knew how to read the river. I looped around where the ice became dangerously clear until I was standing in the center of the frozen river and facing the man from China: a Joseon-*jok*, so he spoke our language. He had an eager smile and a small head—he was small everywhere, it seemed—and he limped slowly forward as if needing my permission to come closer. With every step his left leg swung out rigidly in a semicircle until we faced each other. He was nervous; his right foot kept making circles on the ice behind him like a ballerina.

This man named Seongsik said, "You really do believe me now, don't you? I'm a person who can make these kinds of meetings happen. I know everyone, and everyone knows me. Money? Who needs money? You need connections."

He tore skin from his lower lip with his teeth. He wanted my approval, the way he repeated himself made that clear. But we didn't have much time so I interrupted him.

"I learn fast," I said. "I'll learn anything you want." I shut my eyes tight so I wouldn't have to look at him.

When I opened them, he was still shyly taking me in. The shy ones were the worst, hard to read.

"Why do you want to leave?" he asked, as if half my country, the country of his ancestors, didn't dream of living differently.

I was so nervous that my fingers dug arcs into my palms. "There are no good men in my country."

He brightened as I'd intended. "I'm a good man, I promise."

While the border guard smoked an imported cigarette from the many cases I'd given him to keep him happy, the Joseon man and I hurried through the ten minutes of time we had to talk—the courting time that he had bought for us.

Money was a symbol, a disease that infected our country. It was all the money I had earned after quitting school during the Great Hunger, my life savings you could call it. I was eight when the famine changed everything. After the government rations stopped and the crops were flooded and destroyed year after year, my *eomma* made several trips into China's border towns to find work and food to feed us. Our government had disappeared and everyone who had followed the rules, including my *abba,* died. I didn't follow rules; I stole and bartered and learned quickly, and I survived. But when the government devalued our money and made our savings worthless, all my work became nothing at all. There was no present, and the future looked even worse. Then my monthly bleeding stopped, and I realized I was pregnant.

After that brief meeting, I continued talking with the Joseon stranger on a Chinese Telecom–wired cellular phone that I used to smuggle goods between the two countries. I delayed making decisions while I continued to work and earn yuan. Foreign currency was the only kind I trusted anymore. The same dust clouds blew behind me as I walked to the Chinese border. It opened its large mouth to receive and release dried fish, iron ore, pine mushrooms, and other goods that we floated over in plastic sacks to our Chinese partners across the Tumen River after paying our bribe. Unless we were pretty and poor—then we could pay with our bodies. I stared across the narrow bend of river at the cars and the blue- and red-tiled roofs bright in the sun and imagined who, on the other side, I might become.

There was no dream possible on our side of the river, and a child with only a mother would be a second-class citizen. But I didn't rush and made contact with a broker trolling our border towns for prospective brides to marry unwed Chinese men. This woman with leathery hands approached me at the market, then quickly pulled me away so that we could talk in private and out of danger. She made me offers: "This man they say has one of those wobbly, not so strong hearts, but he's a meek one—so you can do what you want!" "That one's a farmer living in the countryside and owns a lot of livestock." "A landowner—you know what a landowner is, right?" "And this one, this one's a businessman."

"What business?" I asked.

"Business, business," the marriage broker replied, and looked offended.

I thought of telling her about the baby I was carrying, how the man was a powerful local *ganbu* who had protected my growing smuggling business, and laughed out loud.

The businessman could have strange sexual desires or be violent, the farmer could be as old as my grandfather. Rumors traveled through the markets, and I had heard of such marriages. But the harmless-looking man who had arranged our brief meeting a week ago on the frozen river, this sometimes tour guide with his seesaw limp and sun-beaten face, he was real. Even though my *eomma* was famous for not showing until her fifth month, I was afraid my body would start to betray me; leaving wasn't a choice anymore. It was Eomma or my baby.

After the broker that the Joseon man had hired bribed a chain of local officials, after I bribed still others to register me dead of tuberculosis to protect my *eomma,* I left while she was sleeping; it was safer for her not to know much. I packed the essentials, nothing personal, and passed the village walls without looking back. I believed I was good at not looking back.

Maybe it was two or four in the morning when I finally crossed, but all the hours feel the same when you're terrified and ready to end your life if caught. Against the mountain peaks rising like dull knives, the moon stalked our half-naked group wading across the shallow river. The moonlight made us as translucent as ghosts; it was as if we were shedding our very selves to become someone else.

"It'll hurt," the broker leading us out had warned. *Hurt* wasn't the right word for crossing in early spring. Pain needled up my legs. I blew out white clouds too thick, too visible; I tried to stop breathing. Halfway across, I heard what sounded like a gun. We dropped deep into the water, and my hands rose up to beat away a bullet that never came.

Like the thousands before me since the famine, I shadowed the broker's exact watery steps to avoid the mantraps along the shore and the gaze of China's cameras. I could only ask myself: Why didn't I cross before the river's sudden thaw? Finally, shivering, colder than I have ever been, I dragged myself up the muddy bank and kneaded my numb fingers and toes. When I found them still there, I felt light, almost happy. I looked for the man who would be my husband, for now. His thin arms, his chestnut-brown face, anything to reduce the scale of that country suddenly too large for me.

That was how it happened for me, the impossible dream of crossing.

But the Dear Leader's arm had vast reach, and even as I

crossed the river and disappeared to marry the Joseon-*jok* man, we weren't exactly married. We who entered China, and all the children created from these marriages, didn't officially exist.

The broker had received the extra cash that he demanded, and the Joseon man named Seongsik left me overnight at his friend's house. "Only until our wedding," Seongsik said, and blushed.

I was too scared to sleep and too exhausted not to, and my throat was so tight that I couldn't keep my food down. The next day, he returned to gaze at my pale face as if marveling that I was his.

"We're starting out on fertile land, for luck," Seongsik said. I followed him out of the house, fearful that I looked like someone from across the river despite my new clothes. He was referring to the field set up for our wedding ceremony, but when we got there, it looked like nothing could ever grow out of it.

"It's farmed by my church deacon," he said.

The shoes he had me wear, more slender towers than shoes, threatened to send me tumbling into the mud.

"Church?" I didn't know what a church was yet.

He caught me as I wobbled. "Don't worry. Just do what I tell you to." He held me tightly by the arm and pulled me along as if he were leading a cow.

I didn't like being told what to do, but he had paid too large a sum for me. Already twice that morning he worried out loud about the broker's sudden last demands. And I was grateful. How could I not be? Seongsik was as slight as the orphans who snatched corn doughnuts from the hands of customers back home and ate as they were beaten—but he had saved my unborn baby.

I've lived an unusual young life, some would say an extraordinarily difficult life, but I was a typical mother. I had all kinds of dreams for my baby. I had a name picked out if she was a girl and another name picked out if he was a boy, though I was sure she would be a girl. I worried about how her head would emerge from my small body unhurt, how to bathe such a fragile creature. It was the most important thing that had ever happened to me, my living, beating secret that I could share with no one. My baby, only a faint murmur in my belly, but already I felt less lonely.

So I wasn't as frightened as I should have been when the gathering clouds settled over us and Seongsik's people pretended not to stare while they stared at me. Only a man the others called deacon greeted me warmly, clasping his hands around mine.

"You've traveled a long way," he said, though it was only across the river. "You must be tired." Tears crowded my eyes at his hands, their warmth.

A gray-haired matron who smelled of dried mushrooms clutched her purse to her chest as she walked my way, as if I might steal from her.

She said, "It's that awful one-child policy," in informal Korean, as if I were a child she was speaking to or a work hand she had hired. "Perfectly good men like my son have no choice but to marry women like you."

"And what exactly is wrong with someone like me?" I smiled sweetly. The old rag of a woman wouldn't have survived five minutes of my former life.

"Eomeoneem, you promised," Seongsik whined to his *eomma,* suddenly sounding like a ten-year-old. "She's what I want, my Jangmi."

Like that, I was given my new name: Jangmi. Rose, a lovely, thorny name that suited me. So easily, one life ended and another began.

He stroked his *eomma*'s hand, which was rough from farm-work, more in the way of a lover than a son. I didn't like seeing that. No woman wanted her man beholden to his *eomma,* even if she did live far away. He said, "Anyway, she's beautiful like I said, isn't she? I know how to pick them."

"She's too pretty." Her lips pressed together. "Good-looking girls are too demanding."

When you have nothing, you grow up taking. You steal and cheat if you have to. What I knew was that you never got what you wanted if you didn't take it, so I took the first thing I saw: I plucked the pink carnation from my mother-in-law's buttonhole and held it to my nose.

That was the way I was. Not soft, though I looked like I would be soft. I was all gristle and bone and rage. All muscle and metal. I believed I had experienced everything, though I had never been in love.

Numb to pain and fear was how I wanted to be as we drove afterward in a boxy red car to Seongsik's apartment, passing concrete buildings that I couldn't tell apart from one another. The skyline blinded me with its glowing signs—neon, he called it. But it was the hundreds of motorcycles flying past that I couldn't stop staring at. I promised myself that I would become like one of those women who looked so fearless, so free, riding alone on the enormous steel machines.

"Here we are!" Seongsik rushed to open the car door for me.

Dusk reflected off his apartment building and made the windows opaque. This is where you belong, the building's yellow facade seemed to say to me. This is all you're worth, the puddle of urine we passed on the stairwell reminded me. We followed the smoke stains that wound straight up four flights of stairs. All at once the great, terrible China seemed to declare, I'm a building you're unable to leave, and you, you belong to me. I pushed those voices away; I reminded myself that the grim walls only obscured the somewhere beyond. Beyond. It was another name for hope.

I didn't know how to read this world yet. So when Seongsik, still a rabbit-faced stranger to me, opened the front door and the dark hall flooded with chanting, deep and otherworldly, I didn't understand that this was choral music. In the swell of sound that ballooned out of the apartment, I heard the sadness of my *eomma,* my *abeoji.* The people and the past I had abandoned. I fled for the stairs we had just climbed up.

"Where are you going?" He seized me by my hair.

I ripped away from him, my scalp burning. A long coil lay limp in his fist. He forced me to the floor by the shoulders, straddled and pinned me to the cement.

"Where do you think you're going?" he said again.

I pleaded into his face that was tight with disappointment. I choked out, "Don't you hear them? The voices of ghosts?"

For a man like him, the sight of my retreating back must have been the history of all departing women. Only when I kept explaining did he understand that I was running, but not from him.

"I'm sorry, I'm so sorry." He let me go.

Inside the apartment, after he turned the music off and brewed a pot of jasmine tea, he broke the silence. "It's Bach, choral music. I had it set on repeat, for your arrival. Don't be scared."

"Choral music. Bach," I repeated, trying to learn the new world as quickly as I could. One of my hands curved around my unborn baby who would never meet her real *abeoji,* an official, a married man who wouldn't have let her live if he had known about her. I thought about my *eomma* and sank to the couch as far from Seongsik as I could manage. He was as nervous as I was and gripped his teacup as if it were a crowbar.

He gulped down the tea. "Everything in here's quality. I only want the best."

Looking at the man whose square teeth protruded over his lip as he smiled, I wanted desperately to reverse time. To be reborn into a *ganbu*'s family and go to special private schools. Eat red meat every week and enter the University of Pyongyang and never have to think about crossing into China. But my family's lowly *seongbun*—my *abeoji* a coal miner and South Korean relatives staining my *eomma*'s side—meant I was barred from all opportunity. I knew this much: I would be sent to jail or, worse, the camps in the far north if I was caught. The authorities would assume my baby was of impure Chinese blood and murder her.

I moved closer to Seongsik.

He showed off the solid oak furniture and the kitchen counter he claimed competed with the most elite homes in Pyongyang, as if he had personally visited them. The indoor flushing toilet did thrill me, but it was the framed picture of Jesus Christ that I remember most vividly. Why was a white man hanging like a powerful politician in his house? I wondered. I was also intrigued, for this man with a tangled brown beard looked homeless, nothing like the dashing men in the smuggled VCD of *An Officer and a Gentleman,* or the cruel American soldiers in posters stabbing children with bayonets. Not powerful and kind, like the portraits of the Great Leader and the Dear Leader that hung in every house across the river, though even then I thought that a sack of rice was more useful than their portraits. This white man looked weak; he looked so ordinary. So this was the real American!

Seongsik took in all his belongings, including me, and rubbed his stomach as if he were full. "And this is our drinking water," he said in front of a plastic tank standing on four legs.

"What else would you do than drink it—bathe in it?" I said, as if such a machine didn't surprise me.

But when he pressed the blue knob at the top, saying, "Red's for hot, be careful," I wasn't prepared for the water shooting out in a remarkable, reliable stream. It was the promise of better things. My future would begin with this owlish man abandoned by his Chinese wife. My baby would start her life here, and more.

"Your very first electronic piano." Seongsik tapped at the plastic keys.

"Electronic piano," I repeated seriously as if it were new to me, though bands in our country had played the instrument for decades.

"Credit card, sleeping bag, DVD player," I repeated, naming the world that he said was now also mine.

"Look at this, listen to this," he said, and slipped a round disc into yet another machine. I was shocked that everything inside the apartment seemed to require electricity, and even more shocked that electricity continued to surge reliably, the machines buzzing without pause. I was used to black nights, trains idling for days. I began to exclaim when the music silenced me.

The sound reminded me of autumn leaves, drifting currents. Nights while returning home with my goods, afraid of every man I met. There was no fear in that music. Just sadness, and beauty.

"Chopin, one of his nocturnes. Not a scary note in it," Seongsik said. "But you're crying. Oh, why are you crying? I must have hurt you badly!"

"No, it's not that," I said. "I've traveled so far to hear this music."

Another kind of conversation might have happened between us then. For weren't there those cracks in time when life suddenly reversed itself and surprised, and anything became possible? Maybe even a temporary, but real, affection between two strangers who needed each other, for now? But the bedroom door flew open and a young girl emerged from the room, her pink flesh overflowing from the armbands of her nightgown rumpled with sleep.

This girl, who shared Seongsik's squat nose and his anxious, chewed-up lower lip, looked hungrily at him, and he scooped her up in his arms and held her high in the air.

He glowed into her pinched, radish-shaped face. "Is my favorite lady still angry at her *abba*?"

That was when my baby made a whisper of a kick, my stomach flipped, and the overfed girl gave me a murderous look, then wailed, "Abba, you promised!"

4

Yongju

The morning of the last day of my *abeoji*'s life, even the streetlights in our neighborhood were blacked out. After dodging my *abeoji* and in this way proudly refusing the car and driver he made available to me, I walked to the tram in the dark, stopping to write a line of poetry as it came to me. I noticed things that I assumed he wouldn't notice: the smell of burning coal and the grit of soot on my face, how some people wore the bleak dawn like a coat. How in the glass window of the trolley I looked as solemn and awkward as a contrabass, standing a head taller than everyone around me. I listened for the clang of the red and white trolley, watched the traffic girl with her blue and gold cap guide the thin weave of cars, the crumbling plaster of huts tightly packed together that hid behind a front line of apartment buildings. I heard the story of a city being constructed around me, them, all of us, making everyone a part of its story.

I walked with my eyes drawn toward the stray weed, the cigarettes a vendor sold in single units, the older woman lingering alone alongside a bare, cracked wall. Crowds of people talking reminded me of a gaggle of geese honking at one another. I've always been a well-disguised solitary, preferring books to people and music to socializing and playing sports. I didn't see myself as part of any group though I was part of the many that organized our lives, shuttled from place to place in packs, as we all were.

That was how I began the last day of my *abeoji*'s life: dodging encounters with the people closest to me. I arrived at the university and retreated to the back of the class, where I was forgotten, the way I wanted to be. The temperature outside was higher than in the sunless classroom, and all of us were swaddled in winter coats, warming our fingers swollen blue with cold and breathing in the air that caught like glass in our throats.

That evening I returned home from a parade drill, exhausted. For some it was a beautiful spectacle, a point of civic pride, but for me it was only another garish gathering I was forced to participate in. As I took off my shoes, I heard the traditional folk song "Arirang" playing, the kind of music that my modern parents would never listen to in private.

At first I didn't believe what I saw. A stranger was burning photos and documents in our kitchen, standing over a flame that made his cheeks glow yellow and red. "Arirang" continued to undulate through the room. The image enchanted me and from the door I watched the material curl in the wastebasket, until my father's and mother's glossy faces turned to ash and I began to understand. My stomach seized up. The stranger was erasing us.

He looked so ordinary in his black wool coat and suit. He had the tidy haircut I expected for a man of his age, and his diffident air reminded me of someone in a cold office who typed up dull reports all day. I assumed he was half-alive, half-conscious in his environment, as I was, sleepwalking through the orders that had brought him into our house. He looked perplexed as he stared at the fire curling and rising, then looked up at me and pointed at the walls around us. The walls are listening, he meant. I understood immediately.

He said, "You must be back from classes," sounding official and uninterested, unlike his eyes. He made a bowl with his hands, then pointed at the fire. "Where are your parents?"

I said, "I don't know. Working?" I felt strangely calm, as if I were talking about another person in someone else's house.

I trusted that if you did what you were told, you would be left alone, so I went quickly, quietly, to the cabinet and withdrew a large steel bowl, then held the bowl to the faucet and turned the water on at low force so there was no noise. I brought some cornstarch as well. He smothered the fire in the cornstarch and only then drizzled what was left with water. As we watched, a cloud of smoke rose from the charred remains.

"My parents—they . . . they're coming back, yes?" I said. Had they been taken away? My head filled with thoughts and images that I hadn't known were there: the camps farther north of us. The world suddenly much bigger, and lonelier, than I had imagined it.

"Look, you should have a seat." The man's voice was calm, but his hands trembled. "I'm doing a routine inspection," he explained as his eyes danced across the room, landing everywhere but on me. We were not the kind of family used to such inspections.

I waited to discover who the man was and if he had discovered all the usual illegal possessions: shelves of Western VCDs and music, foreign novels and poetry books that were available to select students, questionable gifts that foreign diplomat friends had given my *abeoji* on their trips to the West, and most of all the stacks of foreign currency hidden throughout the house that I had found by accident. When I discovered the false wall built into the closet a few months ago, my mind had begun to spin, uncertain of what else I didn't know.

"My *abeoji* is a loyal, powerful member of the party. There must be some mistake." I picked my words carefully, imagining someone far away listening in. It seemed impossible that a few hours ago I had felt so safe.

"Look at this," I said, and I led him to a letter signed by the Great General. "This is addressed to my *abeoji*. And you know who my *eomeoni* is." Everyone knew who she was.

I anxiously showed him my *abeoji*'s honors and official party photos, a party publication spread out so the Great General's photo was uncreased and turned faceup, and the Great Leader's and the Great General's gleaming portraits prominently placed and dusted daily with a padded stick. All the necessary evidence of a loyal life.

He smiled at me, a thin, sympathetic smile, and I saw that he was afraid for me.

"We have great love and respect for the Great General," I said. "Our entire family does."

I began mourning what I sensed would be the end. Already

the house no longer felt like ours. When our lives were dismantled and taken apart, I wondered who would take my *abeoji*'s grand piano. Or my *eomeoni*'s movie projector. Which anonymous bureaucrat was eyeing which appliance? What else had the stranger burned? I had so many questions that would never be answered. I could only trust him; I had no choice but to trust.

"Of course, of course," the man said. "I know all about your family."

I didn't like that. A blanket of silence fell over us. I looked outside at the street, still icy where our building's shadow fell, and wished my parents were home.

"Look, I have a few questions for you. Again, no one's in trouble. When is your sister coming back?"

Had he read in a file that I had a sister, or was that something he had already known?

He continued. "I'm sure you have studying to do. My son is a good student, he has a head for numbers. You?"

I nodded, and some words fell out of my mouth as terror spread like alcohol through my body. All the abstractions I had seen as someone else's life became real to me.

He cracked the window open, letting the smoke and bitter embers and the scent of burned paper out. A trickle of cold crisp air entered, a girl's thin high call.

He asked me rote questions about my *eomeoni* and *abeoji* as if he was reading from a script. Then he wrote on a notepad and held it up. I'm here to help you, it read. Before I could be sure that I had seen it correctly, he rested the note in the still-smoldering ashes and it shrank and disappeared.

I ran past all that I knew and all that I would forget, past the security guard who suddenly seemed there to keep us in more than to keep others out. I ran, coatless, my fingers icy without gloves, fleeing the image of the man who had left before me. I ran from my brightly lit neighborhood and into the darkness of tram stops and building-size portraits of the smiling Great Leader, past the city's statues and hotel towers, stopping only for a random checkpoint. Ran, feeling a giant beast bearing down on me, though when I turned back there was nothing there. I was afraid of staying in Pyongyang, afraid of leaving. I wished for a power outage to pitch the city into a great unfurling darkness. This was my home, the center of my world, and I couldn't imagine myself banished from it.

Dusk became evening, the time my girl and I had planned to meet at the Pothong River.

I waited for Myeonghui. The wind chilled my sweaty skin as I watched the few out by the riverbank striding back and forth for exercise. This daily life was something that might no longer be mine. My hands knotted tightly together. I was impatient to see Myeonghui. I thought I loved her.

I waited by our designated weeping willow and hummed a few bars of "Whistle," the entire time listening for her. I heard her before I saw her, the way her school uniform made a fine woolen rustle, and her bob swished as she laughed a mild, honest laugh, and shook her head my way as if to say, Not tonight. Though tonight might be all I had left with Myeonghui, whose family had left Japan years ago to return to our homeland. I pulled her closer to my side before the moon could peek out from the clouds and illuminate us to the others.

She swiftly put an arm's width of space between us with her habitual modesty. "You're usually so reasonable, *dongmu*."

I was as intimate with Myeonghui as I had ever been in the time we knew each other. Along the winding river path, I breached the distance between us to brush her wrist, as if touching her would help me recover the order that she was for me. Everything about her was what my family wasn't: relentlessly formal, a clarity to her quietness that helped me hear her heavy skirt sway like a bell. I wonder what she meant to me, if she had mattered to me only because I knew her family's ties to Japan would have enraged my *abeoji,* whose own *abeoji* had been murdered by Japanese colonialists. Anyone with Japanese associations was considered unsafe, suspicious.

Again, she moved out of my reach. Only she was betrayed by her eager left foot skipping ahead of her eager right, her breath catching in a rhythm common to those who had come from Japan, the trace of the past echoing on her tongue.

That night there was no family, no committee duties, no small group studies, and few words spoken between us, which meant fewer lies to protect each other and our families. There was only the time given us. We avoided the occasional passing bike, a drunk man stumbling home. The distant conversations of other strollers murmured around us like restless ocean waves, overlapped and blurred into each other, until for a moment I heard only our small voices ballooning in the emptiness.

"You're so lovely," I said. It was true, though in the dark she was a faint outline, an occasional flash of skin so bone white her arms gleamed. You didn't have to see beauty to know it was there.

She said, "You're so quiet tonight . . . so strange . . ."

I turned toward her voice. She sensed the fine difference between my normal quiet and brooding, and knew me without knowing anything about me.

"We've known each other so long now, and it seems wrong that we know so little about each other. You feel so unreal in the dark, as if you were never there."

"No, no, *ireobseubnida*." She laughed, her hair flying in the air as she shook her head. "We have time."

She swung her slender arms from side to side, her faith in the future intact. Again that pause, and in it began the kinds of silent conversations that none of us dared to have with each other. In those imagined conversations, she told me what it meant to have Japanese soil in her. I confessed what I feared might be happening to my family.

I watched her whirl and embrace the moon's silhouette, and for the first time I thought she must carry with her an unlived life and the sadness of her family.

I asked, "How did it feel on . . . on the last day of your life?"

"*Dongmu!* You're so morbid, thinking about death already."

"I don't mean dying—not exactly. But when your family . . . left. Being dead, but not dead. Only . . . gone."

Her hands dropped and her voice took on a clipped formality. "I don't understand you today."

I thought about all the things that could go wrong when you tried to cross into China.

I said, "Too much of us can't be measured. When Abeoji plays the piano, each time he plays, the phrasing is more or less the same. Recognizable, is what I mean. You can listen to one recording and compare it to another, but it's the same composition. It's not like people—we're so different from moment to moment that we wouldn't be recognizable if we didn't have this body and voice, these enormous fingerprints."

I kept speaking nonsense, anything to defend myself from my thoughts. Were traitors actually traitors, or were they wronged, betrayed, or just unlucky? My laugh grew into painful, unstrung sounds.

Myeonghui pulled away. "Someone might hear," she said with the same pleasant, even tone.

Without warning, she added, "*Dongmu,* don't do anything you can't reverse. It's best you not say anything more."

I weighed whether to return home or run away, though how and to where was beyond my ken. I thought of my *dongsaeng,* only thirteen, at home alone and waiting until I returned to have dinner. I was afraid. For the first time, I pulled Myeonghui close to me with my arm around her waist the way Jack had done to Rose on the sinking *Titanic.* Like a girl raised properly, she resisted this first embrace, then gradually gave in. Of course this must be love, I thought, giving my nostalgia and fear and longing for all I was about to lose a name.

Much later I heard the stories of others: older women who recalled the seven years they dated their husbands before permitting a peck on the cheek; a receptionist at the Koryo Hotel who relived the illegal kiss she shared with an English teacher from Canada, who had, before he left forever, bequeathed her his final, stingy gift of loneliness. But that night there was only the way I cleaved to Myeonghui.

My right hand was a feathery pressure on her hips; my lips memorized her eyes, her nose, her lips. And though she was a proper girl from a good family, she sensed the strangeness of the night and allowed my arms to embrace her collarbone like a necklace. She must have known we were saying good-bye. This first kiss would remind me, whenever my hometown seemed an impossible dream, of who I had been.

5

Jangmi

Seongsik's daughter was eight years old, the same age I'd been when I quit school as the famine swept through our country. That first day when he tried to show me the bedroom, Byeol stretched her arms and legs across the width of the door frame and blocked me from passing.

"Where are you going?" she cried. "That's where Abba and I sleep."

It was the only other room in the apartment. I was relieved, the dreaded inevitable moment postponed. Seongsik lifted his daughter up again from behind, so her arms and legs as round as Pyongyang dumplings spun in the air. He said, "Now, we've talked about this."

The girl lurched backward as Seongsik struggled to hold her. I remembered being eight again and became afraid. I had licked the last of the ground-up cornmeal and bark from my bowl, then ate from my *eomma*'s bowl as well. She had let me. My schoolteachers began stealing food instead of coming to school, and our family cracked open like an egg. After Abba died, Eomma left our one-room row house and went to China for the first time, and I sulked behind my aunt's back so I wouldn't cry. I tried to hide how afraid I was of never seeing her again. I remember needing her. I remember loving her.

Would I be a good *eomma*? Was anyone ever capable of being a good *eomma*? The girl called Byeol—a strange name, a star in the night sky—had uneven bangs that her father must have cut for her, and those bangs touched me. I decided I would cut the girl's hair next time.

I gave her hair a light stroke, so as not to scare her.

"I had lice last week," Byeol said. "Really bad. These tiny white bugs were crawling all over the comb." I removed my hand.

Seongsik put her down. "You going to behave?"

She ran into the bedroom and flopped on the bed. "This is my room."

"All right, we'll sleep together, just for tonight. I'll spread a *yo* on the floor." He sighed. "Remember, she's only eight. You know what eight is like."

I was grateful, and relieved, when Byeol jumped up and down on the large raised bed, refusing to leave us alone. The bed was lined with a hospital ward's worth of dolls, some missing an arm or a leg, one headless, another bald. She snatched the one intact doll with straw-colored hair and breasts shooting out like rockets and held the doll's lips to her ear. She peered over its head at me.

"She says she doesn't like you," she said. "She says none of them like you. They were going to throw them out—they didn't have a home," she sang as she jumped in circles around her *abba,* marking her territory. "I rescued them. Kind of like Abba rescued you."

You couldn't say something like that to an *eoreun;* I was over twice her age. It was as if she had slapped me. I understood she was threatened by me, but I couldn't even reprimand her; I had no such power. All I could do was wait and see what my new husband would do.

Seongsik looked from me to his daughter. He combed his fingers through his hair so roughly it looked as if he would rip out what was left.

"I've got the money to buy her new dolls, I do, but the church insisted," he said, and fled the room.

Once he left, a spring came loose and my body became alert and capable. The walls were only walls, the dolls only dolls. The girl flopped backward onto the thin mattress and pretended to sleep, but I squatted down to her level.

"If you make it difficult for me, it will also become difficult for you." I kept my voice light, friendly. "But it doesn't have to be that way. We can get along. I can be a nice person, really. You might even like me."

"You're not a nice person, I can tell," the girl said flatly.

"You don't know me." My eyes crowded with tears, but I didn't let them fall. "You don't know how I've suffered."

"I am nice. Everyone says so. I look like my *eomma.*"

"Are you being nice to me, Byeol? What do you think? I'm not trying to replace your *eomma.* I want us to be friends."

Byeol only made dizzying circles on her back, making a mess of the bed.

"Lots of people are nice to me, almost everyone I meet."

I leaned in until our noses nearly touched and said gently, "There is always an exchange between people, and right now that exchange is between you and me. It's your choice. It can be easy or it can be hard, but I want it to be easy for both of us."

The girl sat up, her lips pursed into a stubborn knot that mirrored her father's. "What about my *abba* and you? What does he get, when you're only a North Korean?"

I straightened. I was sure that men wanted only one thing.

"Don't worry about your *abba*," I said. "He knows what he wants."

Seongsik surprised me the next morning, tucking a dethorned red rose behind my ear. "A rose for a Rose," he said, blushing like a boy.

He hadn't told me about Byeol's existence, but he was a romantic. He insisted on music to match the mood of the weather and the light of the day, and he announced Classical! Rock! K-pop!, changing the small discs as each piece startled me with its strangeness. I wondered how many months he had replayed these scenes to himself since his wife had left him, living alone with an imaginary woman he courted nightly in the dark. He was so eager to love me, this man, and I was prepared to use that love.

Before dinner he told me to fold my hands together while he conducted a conversation with someone who wasn't there. I finally found the courage to ask about the American bastard framed and hanging above the television, and he said, "That's

Jesus Christ," with reverence in his voice. Only then did I connect his monologue to the air with the picture. "God's son who gave up his life for us."

"Jesus Christ?"

"Jesus, Jesus," said Byeol, suspicious. "You mean you don't know Jesus Christ?"

She pushed a plate of bean sprouts my way, then gave me a strange look when I pushed it back toward her. The smell was too strong for me. Seongsik retrieved a large black book and placed it in my hands as if offering me a letter signed by the Great Leader himself.

"It's the Bible," he said. "It's the only book we need."

I flipped the book open and traced the lines across the page.

He was so eager that he leaned toward me until his shirt touched his rice and told me that the son of God could walk on water and multiply five loaves of bread and two fish into a plentitude that fed entire villages.

I wondered if my new husband was sick or prone to imaginative spells.

"Has anyone seen this man do it—walk on water?"

He regarded me with fatherly amusement. "You'll grow to have faith."

He lectured me on how unholy my country was. While he drew circles in his daughter's bowl of rice with chopsticks, he spoke of famine and poverty and what it did to people, as if he had crossed the river and personally witnessed it. He wondered out loud how we lived without technology. What he said wasn't untrue, not exactly. Even after all the honest and rule-abiding ones had died in the famine, most still experienced winter hungers that gnawed at the stomach, then ate what they could in the summer. Too many of us knew violence and corruption and the addiction of homegrown *bbindu,* our medicine that I later learned was called opium, which helped you forget about food. But the way he looked at me as he spoke from some high-up place offended me. It was as if I were being branded as a North Korean, part of a mass of people who were all the same.

I said, "I've eaten meat more than a few times, and always had money to buy cold buckwheat noodles at the market."

I took delicate bites on purpose, my mouth hardly moving, while his rotated from side to side like an ox's. Maybe I hadn't had much schooling, I added, but I knew my letters and had owned a cellular phone and a stiff silk *hanbok.* A friend had once given me a gold watch as a gift.

"Gold? Real gold?" He spat out a mouthful of rice onto the table. "Your friend's a man."

The girl screamed, "A man?" as if her father was exempt from this category.

"If he treated you so great, why didn't you marry him?"

I wondered if his jealousy could be useful to me.

"It was my uncle," I said at last.

He leaned in closer. "You can tell me anything." He was testing me. I had been tested before. "You don't have to hide from me."

I didn't forget to compensate him with a kiss.

His daughter and I shared the bedroom after her *abba* was called by "one of his associates" to guide a Christian group touring through the Yanbian province and had to leave for a few days. Anything that delayed my first night alone with him was good news.

"I'm entrusting Byeol to you," he said. "She never recovered after her *eomma* left."

His guide work had forced him to travel around the region, leaving Byeol at the mercy of his local Christian friends. But now he had me. Our marriage was also practical.

I linked my arm in his. "You can trust me, I took care of my *abba* until the very end. I know how to take care of people."

He crouched over the black and white tiles of the kitchen, digging up a book of recipes. "You know, I try to get the tourists to help your people at their hideouts. Some live for years in underground caves like moles." There was sympathy in his voice but also a vein of satisfaction in telling me this.

My name is Jangmi now, I reminded myself the next morning as I made his prescribed breakfast for Byeol. But one bite of the salted mackerel that I had been craving sent me gagging to the bathroom. The girl noticed, how could she not? She watched everything I did. I told her I had a chronically weak stomach. That morning, I learned that unlike my *eomma,* I wasn't immune to morning sickness.

When the girl left for school, I tried to better understand the man I had married and went through his belongings—as his wife, I considered this fair—and saw the care that Seongsik had taken. He had set up a new life for me in the common room: a stack of Chinese language books and CDs with a note to me taped to the top cover, even a glass ball that rained snow on a

couple when you shook it. I had never seen an object so beautiful.
I flipped through his shelf and, for a few hours, skimmed the
books and magazines in our language—a language that was the
same but different somehow, pages with words I had never seen
and alien expressions. I looked up the many words I didn't know
as I read, and was stunned at what they said about our Dear
Leader—Japanese sushi the price of a car for a dinner party,
women my age dancing naked in front of him—stories I dis-
missed as Western lies. I tried to study Chinese, but how could I
when there was so much to discover in magazines and on television? I had a television for the first time in my life.

I wanted to buy everything. I learned there was an ink to make
your eyelashes thicker and longer, and that this was supposed to be
attractive. You could have your legs operated on and made thinner
in South Korea, endless tubes of color could transform anyone into
a beauty. I paid attention. I wanted a life beyond marrying a man
who offered so little. I tried hard not to think about my *eomma*
squatting at the market selling potato and corn cakes—how would
she survive without me? Would the official report of my death keep
her safe from questioning? Would Seongsik accept the baby as his,
at least for the time we had together? How would I escape this marriage and find my way to Nam Joseon, a country that Seongsik called
South Korea? Smuggled VCDs had showed me that in Nam Joseon,
South Korea, whatever its name, scrawny women owned rooms
heaped with clothes and cars with heated seats. A safe country.

By the afternoon, I found myself eager for his sour-faced
daughter to return home from school.

When Byeol opened the door, bringing the early smells of

spring with her, I offered her baked sweet potatoes to snack on and asked, "Do you need help with your homework?"

Dots of red spread, like bloodstains, across her cheeks. "I never need help."

Everyone needs an *eomma,* Seongsik had said with an expectant look, but the way the girl's face drained of sunshine when she saw me made it clear that she was not that kind of daughter. Still, an hour later as she read to her broken dolls, I thought, My baby must be a girl.

I tapped on her book. "Our lovely girl, what would you like for dinner?"

She smiled sweetly and asked for fish again.

"Wouldn't you like *bibimbap* instead?" I had seasoned and cooked mixed vegetables while she was at school, checking my reaction to the different root vegetables.

"I want fish. Abba told you my favorite food is fish." She kicked her tiny schoolbag across the floor and looked prepared to kick me next. "All I ever want is grilled fish."

So I made her the grilled fish, breathing through my mouth and hardly able to look at the gills and silver ribbons of skin that I had once hungered for. I turned the dead creature from one side to the other, expecting it to flop over and gaze at me with its bulging eyes. When I wouldn't eat it, she looked triumphant, though she clearly had no idea what she had won.

He was damaged goods; I should have known as much. At the time, it shocked me to see such misery even across the border.

When he returned home after several nights away, the dreaded event happened. He bribed Byeol with sweets and successfully lured her to a *yo* spread out on the common-room floor, then he stood by the bed and stripped off his slacks and striped sweater, finally ready to claim his reward. Clothed, he had looked like the shabby men from my hometown. But naked, he was half man, half machine. His right leg was kept intact with a leather garter belt, and beneath the thigh, a metal leg ran down to a steel ankle and ended with a foot in the shape of a shoe. This wasted leg thrust forward in my direction like a challenge. I tasted the metal in my mouth. I shouldn't have been surprised; what kind of man married a fugitive from the country across the river, with no rights and no money, forced to live on his fickle mercy? The silence between us filled with what we thought we knew about each other.

"I guess it comes off?" I said jauntily. I approached and sat at the bed's edge.

He gave me a smile like dried seeds. I patted his knee. Its strange, hollow sound made me jump.

He nodded. "You can rely on me," he said, and made a sound between a gasp and a sob. "Everyone likes me. I may not be much to look at, but they know I'm a good man. It takes time, but maybe you'll like me, too. And I'm very clean and I'm a good cook." Despite myself, I felt sorry for him.

"Well, then. You don't always go to bed with it on, do you?"

"All right, then," he said. "All right."

He took it off. He held the fake leg in the air and asked me to set it beside the bed. The leg made a dull thud.

"You walk on it all day and the pain goes all the way up." He spoke slowly now. "You're not afraid?"

"I'm not scared. I don't scare easily. It was only startling."

"I'm damaged goods, I know," he said. It embarrassed me to hear my thoughts echoed. He stroked the remains of his right leg. "I'm sorry."

"You had an accident."

"I wasn't always not there!" He stroked the end of his thigh. "I lost it in a factory. In South Korea. I went there to make money—all the healthy Joseon-*jok* in China leave to make money if they can—but I came back with debts and one leg.

"South Korea, it's war there. A bad, bad country." He frowned as if the country of wealth and opportunity had deliberately deprived him of his leg.

"Come closer," he said, though I couldn't get much closer.

His gaze slid away from me as if he required permission to look, so I unzipped my dress and unclasped my bra and revealed myself under the hard fluorescent light. He couldn't stop looking now. I needed his looking. For him to become the father to my baby. I took his hand and planted it on the curve of my breast. It was dangerous not to encourage him. He stared downward; I kept my eyes fixed ahead and waited.

6

Danny

The morning after I'd nearly drowned, I woke up to my nose filled with the familiar smells of frogs and lizards preserved in formaldehyde. My own bedroom. My eyes still closed, I tried to block out other thoughts by reciting the order of my books lining my three shelves—one-third Mandarin, one-third Korean, one-third English—then the names of the beloved finger puppets I'd made myself, until the alarm clock rang and I hit it before the cuckoo bird said "cuckoo."

It was no good. It was still Sunday, I'd still been rescued lying facedown in the water the day before with only my mind sinking to an imaginary bottom. I'd turned myself into a public fool. Tomorrow was still Monday, which meant school. I got up and knocked down my academic awards from the walls, pulled my clothes lined up from light to dark from their hangers, then collapsed onto the bed. The mess didn't change anything. I was still me.

The dark living room I marched through was part of a

double-car garage converted into what was probably the smallest house in Loma Linda. Since my mom left on the church mission, he'd swept all her potpourri, porcelain figurines, and other pretty collections into Costco boxes, which he'd stacked in the closet, leaving our house as bare as a box, the way he liked it. The coffee-stained carpet and the dorm-room disrepair left by the families before us looked even sadder than before, a place any sane person would want to leave.

I was startled and sorry when I saw my dad in the kitchen. He had a five o'clock shadow and was wearing the same plaid shirt and pants he'd had on the day before. This was the man who rarely let me hug him because of the potential exchange of germs. I had done this to him.

I said, "Morning, Dad."

His eyes stayed fixed on the sizzling tofu in the pan as he muttered to himself, "Time made man and man made God to help him understand time."

He set down orange juice in front of me and a plate of tofu with scallions and garlic, stir-fried in his special sauce.

"Look, I have a plan," he said.

"Thanks, Dad." I immediately began eating, my mind solely on the prospect of school. On Monday. The day before, when I'd made a one-man show of myself to all of Bible camp, seemed a mere preview of what awaited me.

I kept my mouth full of food, my head low to the plate. I waited for him to ask me about the day before, dreaded it, in fact, and it seemed he was waiting for me to explain. The soft wedges of tofu caught in my throat. How could I tell my dad that he had an idiot of a son who'd nearly drowned with his life vest on? How did you explain that?

When I finally did look up, he was gazing at the flat California sunshine coming in through the window, poking between his teeth with a green plastic toothpick. He sawed it back and forth, then cleared his throat. His eyebrows knitted together and he turned his milky brown eyes on me.

"Maybe it's because we never gave you brothers or sisters," he said. "I'm very aware that I've failed you as your *abba* in some way or other, and I'm not confident that I have the skills to make the necessary amends."

I was so surprised that I didn't know how to respond, and I always had a response.

"Frankly, your mother was an accident in my life, having a child was an accident. I suspect Mother Nature meant for me to be a bachelor. I'm not good at this."

I knew that any topic that diverged from fact made him more uncomfortable and awkward than he already was, but something still collapsed inside me. "So you regret having me."

"Don't be immature, Daehan," he said sharply. "I want you to be safe. But you clearly aren't well here. There's no reason you should feel well here, with me."

His facial expression didn't change once.

"Well, you're getting your wish. You're going to China for a few weeks. It'll be good for you. I thought about it for a long time last night and purchased an airline ticket online for you, Beijing onward to Yanji. I'll call your *eomma* once she's back from her work trip. You'll be better off with her."

It was a trip I'd fantasized about for years; I also felt rejected. What was worse, we weren't the kind of family who could afford last-minute airline tickets. I wondered what meager savings account he'd broken into.

"So you're going to send me away. Get rid of the problem."

"But you wanted to go!" He scrubbed at his face with his knuckles. "It'll be good for you, time to rest and recover. Help us, help your parents. Why can't you be a good, normal kid?" he said sadly, as if normal wasn't what I keenly wanted to be.

He began clearing the table, then turned back with a plate balanced in each hand. "I want to know one thing. Did you think about us at all when you jumped? One thought about your parents, what it would do to us?"

"Dad, it was an accident. I wasn't trying to do what you think! It wasn't like that, I promise!"

As I tapped my glass with the fork, the stubborn rhythm of his voice thinned out for me. *Ping! Ping!* The bright notes lifted my spirits, lifted me out of the kitchen, to elsewhere. After all, elsewhere had to be better than here.

Over the next few days, I made meticulous preparations. I packed my Chinese passport; I raided my beloved survival kit and withdrew my Leatherman Squirt PS4, not much bigger than a toothpick; a Bic pen sawed in half to save weight and a notebook the size of my palm; a multi-use plastic bag that served as a tent, SOS signal marker, and hydro bag; a military meal kit; a parachute cord, the sturdiest of ropes; vitamins and a sleeping aid; two changes of clothes. On my person, I would keep a money wallet stitched into my underwear, zip-up military Gore-Tex combat shoes and all-terrain tiger-striped military pants—the basic pattern American soldiers donned during Vietnam. Once packed and prepared, I felt more secure. A few days later, armed with my supplies snugly fit into a backpack and a suitcase of goodies for my mom, we left the house at sunrise.

The streetlights flickered on and off as our car curved away from Loma Linda. Good-bye to the neighborhood's manicured lawns, the thick blanket of smog, to my teachers' and school counselors' expectations, to the habit of excelling. I couldn't even remember why I had wanted to go to Harvard. I felt buoyant as we drove past a grove of corporate-owned orange trees that seemed to stand between me and a new life. China. The word rolled off my tongue. My backpack bounced on my back. It was happening, it was real. I was crossing borders for the second time in my life. I believed I was prepared.

I often think about borders. It's hard not to. There were the Guatemalans and Mexicans I read about in the paper who died of dehydration while trying to cross into America. Or later, the Syrians fleeing war and flooding into Turkey. Arizona had the nerve to ban books by Latino writers when only a few hundred years ago Arizona was actually Mexico. Or the sheer existence of passports, twentieth-century creations that decide who gets to stay and leave.

Borders aren't a random obsession of mine—unlike my affection for the double helix or Burmese temples—since they'd already changed my life. My family was Joseon-*jok,* ethnic Koreans who'd lived alongside the Han Chinese in northeastern China. That is, except during the madness of China's Cultural Revolution when my grandfather crossed into North Korea, where my mom was born. If my mom and her family hadn't recrossed while they still could, I might have been born in North Korea. As it was, I still had relatives on both sides of the river, and having grown up in northeastern China until I was nine, I could pass for a North Korean from the Hamgyong region when I spoke Korean, like many in the Chinese border towns.

Still, when the plane landed in Yanji and I didn't see my mom anywhere, I felt disoriented. The airport's fluorescent yellow and blue plastic chairs, the glass-walled facade, the tidal wave of concrete wasn't the China of my memory. I felt, suddenly, American, though my only passport was Chinese.

The ground tipped as I scanned the pointillist painting of black-haired heads before me. I blamed jet lag for the vertigo of crossing, for that shift when language jostled out of place, and my mind sought to reverse the order of words in my head and became part of another geography again. Thankfully, I remembered that I was supposed to call my parents with my phone card once I landed. Plans, another anchor.

My mom didn't pick up the phone, but my dad answered in one ring. He said, "You haven't met Ku *ajeoshi* yet?"

"Ku *ajeoshi*?"

"Eomma must have lost her cell phone on her last work trip, but I'd already bought the plane ticket." He took a deep breath. "I didn't want to worry you."

He told me that this Mr. Ku, his old school friend, was holding a sign with my name on it. He would drive me all the way to my mom's town. I felt dismayed. There was little worse than hours of interrogation by a stranger who acted like he knew you, so I insisted on being dropped off at the bus station. It was my hometown, too, and a small one at that. My dad objected.

"Half the people in town know us," I said. "I'll be fine."

"You're not going unescorted for a minute, after what you did."

"Dad, I've taken survival tests and camped across half the Sierra Nevada practically alone. And I'm of legal age to drive a car, pilot a glider, even get married. I'll be more than fine."

When a dot of a man across the hall waved at me and started walking my way, I pretended to give in but began drafting plans. After years of surviving American public schools, I was pretty fearless.

"Daehan!" The man, whose upper torso reminded me of an Asian Santa Claus, and the lower, a sparerib, thumped me on my back as if he was my friend. "I haven't seen you since you used to spit on your favorite foods, so no one else could have any of it. I'll never forget how you sucked your toes, too."

"All babies do that."

He laughed. "You were six. Not exactly a baby."

It didn't get any better in the eatery we settled into. Mr. Ku was even more heavy-handed with the memories than I'd expected. Halfway through breakfast, I said I needed the bathroom, which was located conveniently on the building's second floor, and gave him the slip. I tucked a note of apology under the car's window wipers before jumping on the first local bus heading out of town that passed me, avoiding the central bus station. Wherever I ended up, I trusted I could eventually transfer to the one I needed since buses were a way of life in China.

I transferred onto a second bus, then later a third. I kept my feet a safe distance from my seat partner's chicken, which was squashed into a cage. "I'm going home," I whispered. "I'm finally going home."

My hometown wedged in a forgotten corner of China felt like it belonged to another self. After six years away, its buildings seemed to me as plain as the people, worn out like saggy granny panties. On the main strip there were song rooms, bars, and clubs with Korean signs in neon displayed above the scarlet-red Chinese characters. It was hard to imagine my bow-and-arrow-gripping ancestors roaming these stark mountains and plains, a fact that China tried hard to ignore so that it could claim the land had always been theirs. Or to imagine North Korea's so-called Great Leader journeying through the land with his bandit group of rebels and first wife in tow, on his way to Russia. Those times must have required desperate courage.

I hitched up my belt, heavy with emergency rations of dried tofu and nuts, bought a chunk of fresh tofu from a vendor, and bargained with a cyclo driver. When he tried to rip me off, I began walking toward my mom's apartment through the landscape of comforting faces that looked so similar to mine.

I headed down a ventricle of paved streets in the town—there were more than I'd expected—and mapped a grid of old apartments in my head as I walked. I passed snack stalls, corners where kids might target the ones in uniforms from better schools and, just maybe, target me. I sampled dumplings, spun sugar, and grilled chicken on a stick until my mouth flooded with the tastes of my childhood. The crowd thickened and thinned around me like oil. I passed twelve people treading by slowly, nine trotting onward rapidly, approximately one out of five of them wearing lace-up shoes. I dodged a car that rumbled onto the sidewalk and had to dart into an outdoor market when I saw the owner of a Han Chinese restaurant that my family knew. Inside, I observed a moment of silence for seven slaughtered carcasses of pigs. Finally, I felt it: the thrill of being out of my time line, in China, a body returning to the past to escape the past.

After asking for directions from a few people, sometimes in Mandarin and sometimes in Korean, I arrived exhausted at my mother's building.

The low-rise apartment building was covered in dirty yellow tiles and laid out in a Soviet-style grid. I walked past men playing mahjong in the lobby, their syllables like music to me, up to the fourth floor until I was standing at her door that was covered with bright scarlet and gold ads. All my rehearsed speeches morphed into uncertainty. Chances were high that my mom wouldn't be happy with me. After all, I was half the reason they'd left for America in the first place. I pressed the buzzer and waited. I was desperate for simple solutions. My mom, keeper of the family flame, our rainmaker and solution seeker, chair of all committees, would diagnose what was wrong with me.

She called out from the apartment, "Who is it?"

I called back, "A hundred-and-fifty-pound surprise in his favorite military fatigues!"

Feet battered the floor behind the front door, other doors opened and slammed, as if a dozen people were moving under my mom's orders. When the door finally opened and I presented myself to her like a birthday present, my mom squinted through the gap in the door as if trying to decide who I was.

She still looked as old-fashioned as an apple but had changed somehow. It was as if the geography had renewed her. Her short hair had grown out long and feminine, her nails were polished, and the perfume of honeysuckle instead of rice crackers wafted from her. I became worried as frown lines deepened between her eyes. Only when she threw her arms open wide did her mom face—there were no other words for it—finally assert itself.

"My Dumbo! My Daehan!" Her smile was bright, her voice loud enough to wake up statues. "*Naeh ahdeul!*"

Naeh ahdeul. My son. Those words made me ache. She tugged at my ears. "My wonderful Dumbo, you must be a ghost because my *ahdeul* is in America. How did you get here? How did you ever find me?"

"The miracle of technology and a little tenacity," I said. It was clear that Dad hadn't been able to reach her yet.

As we walked inside, words came tumbling out of me. I rattled on about the horrific airplane food, how I'd learned to make four new sailing knots on the flight over, how I'd lost my map and didn't know what to do with myself anymore. I told her about my epic journey to her door and that I couldn't bear the inanity of school anymore and wanted to figure things out. I said that Dad kept forgetting to water the plants so even the cacti would have died without my intervention, that I was sorry but I'd stopped practicing the violin the day she left for the airport.

"Lots of high schoolers are still stuck at the id stage of development," I said. "The word *cool* should be banned from the dictionary." I told her I missed her.

She gave my ear a hard, loving tug. "Did you eat? You need some stew, or dumplings. There's nothing good here. But your favorite eatery—Songbokui's—is still open. And the same woman's there, the one with the dyed red hair you were always trying to learn recipes from when you were too small to reach the stove."

"All I've been doing today is eating," I said. "But I'd give up a kingdom for some juice or milk."

I didn't add it up, her quick, nervous speech, the way she'd blocked the door until I squeezed in past her, and the jittery way she steered me into the kitchen, rushed me through a glass of orange juice, then steered me right back to the common room. Not yet. I was too busy taking in her pale pink slippers, the table with cat claws for legs, a purple vase on top of it. The space with its feminine airs was so different from the darkness that I'd left behind. I was happy to see her well settled and devoted to her work, but I also resented how she had managed to make a bright, cheerful life without us.

"How is your father, that silent, no-talk man? Still all laughs?"

The way she said it—as if he were some man from her distant past, a silly man safe to mock—made me feel protective of him.

"He's doing all right. Still discovering the universe in a stop-watch. He misses you, you know."

"Daehan, now, you know what I'm going to ask you." She pulled on a down jacket. "It's dangerous, the way you are. Why are you suddenly here in the middle of the school semester and how did you get here? How could your *abba* not tell me you were coming?"

"It was Abba's idea." I told her it wasn't exactly his fault and that he had tried calling her several times after he'd bought the ticket, which was when I learned that she had suddenly ditched her cell phone.

"There were work problems." Her jaw went tight. "How can that man pull you out of school one day and send you across the globe without checking with me first?"

So much had happened in the few days we hadn't talked and I didn't know where to start. The suicide attempt that wasn't actually a suicide attempt didn't seem like a good place to begin, and I wasn't ready to tell anyone about Adam. She ruffled my hair as if I were a surly poodle that required humoring. She knew me better than anyone else and normally would have questioned me with a sushi knife's precision, sensing that something was wrong.

Instead she said, "Let's get something to eat," and didn't listen when I told her once more that I'd already eaten a camel's weight in food.

"Come on, put on your shoes," she said. "What if I hadn't been at home? I can't believe your *abba*."

The unfamiliar helium in her voice left me dazed. Her behavior, flying from one world and landing in another, all of it unsettled me.

"How rash of him." She began to sniffle. "Something terrible could have happened to you."

"I won't go back, Mom." That one sentence came out in English.

"After a few weeks here, you'll come to your senses. You can do anything with that wonderful brain God has given you—I won't let you ruin it," she said, and slipped into black flats. "Goodness, I have so much to do and now I'll be worrying half the time about you."

That was when I heard a cough.

It was a small apartment; there weren't many places to hide. I headed in the direction of the cough and opened the bedroom door, but there was no one there.

"Who is it?" I said. "Who's here?"

My mother seized me by my shoulders, trying to pull me out of the room, but I had shot up in the past year and I pulled away and flung open the wardrobe doors one by one.

Behind one of them was a man. Deacon Shin from our church in California, folded up like a broken chopstick and squeezed in between my mom's dresses. The severe-looking, graying man with round eyeglasses didn't look so different from my dad, but he was crucially not my dad. A man who was talkative and sang solos in the choir, who was the first to rescue a cat stuck in a tree and volunteer to flip burgers at church barbecues. A man not my dad, but a man who had somehow become closer to my mom than my dad. Nearly five thousand miles closer. An arm's length closer. The other life beyond the missionary work.

Deacon Shin released a long, painful breath. He said, "Daehan."

"I can explain," my mom said, as if there were any possible legitimate explanations for our church deacon hiding in her closet.

I ran out of the bedroom. The hypocrisy, it was too much for me.

I don't remember how I wiggled out of my mother's grip and spun past her. I don't remember where I struck her to get away or in which exact moment I understood that the read-a-book-in-bed companionship that my dad offered wasn't enough for my mom. I remember Deacon Shin immobile in the closet, his lips kissing his knees, how my mother's voice cracked as she called out my name. I remember how the walls and door of my mom's bedroom seemed to part for me but not how my hiking boots magically appeared on my feet.

She reached for me, saying my name. I fled down the stairs, skipping steps as the patter of my mom's feet followed me down.

7

Yongju

Even back then I had a vague understanding that our country was no stranger to hunger. I knew that some hungered for what was known: noodles in steaming anchovy broth, the food rations that had stopped for most people years ago, the security of orderly routines. Others hungered for things they'd seen in bootlegged South Korean television shows: heating in winter, glamour, chocolate cream pies that came individually wrapped like birthday presents. Then there were hungers that I hadn't dared to hunger for. Freedom to travel. Freedom from surveillance, from fearing that what you said and did was being watched and that someday you would be questioned about it. Now a strange new hunger invaded me. Where, I wondered, as we drove past bare blue mountains in the Toyota truck that picked us up outside the city, where was Abeoji?

"Mr. Rhee is going on a business trip north, and he is kind enough to take us where we need to go," Eomeoni said, as if it wasn't four in the morning.

My *dongsaeng*'s teeth chattered so violently she couldn't speak. Her face matted with dried tears made me feel even more helpless; I could do nothing for her. Instead of our *abeoji,* the stranger I had found in our apartment was driving us up as far north as he was able, where, I guessed, we would be met by another car. This man, who had swiftly arranged this late-night disappearance over the last few hours, was more powerful, more resourceful than I'd thought.

I knew and Eomeoni knew and the man knew that his name wasn't Mr. Rhee and that this business trip was a lie so extravagant it wasn't worth telling. I wondered who had been paid off and what fortune exchanged for our escape, and how the man had managed to extricate Eomeoni from wherever she was being held. Most of all, I wondered what had happened to our *abeoji*.

The man didn't turn to glance at us, either so intent on the dirt road ahead or afraid to let us see his face, as if his expression would betray too much. But to my *eomeoni* he said, "Are you warm enough?" with such tenderness, it was as if his voice were stroking her hand and trying to calm her. It didn't matter to me that she responded to his quiet anguish with distant, measured gratitude. I knew then that they cared about each other.

It was too much: the sudden flight, the amorphous shape of the future, the revelation of my mother's lover. Or at least a man who loved her enough to pay enormous bribes and put himself in danger, a man she might have loved back if she weren't a married woman.

I leaned over the passenger seat up front. "How do you know each other?"

Eomeoni turned back to me, her face hidden beneath a rough woolen hood I'd never seen before. "We were childhood friends," she said. "You shouldn't even know that much."

"Does that mean you've been in contact all this time?"

"He's helping us at great risk when no one else can! Don't ask an older person such questions. I didn't raise you that way."

"It's all right," he said. "The poor kids."

And just as I was about to ask what I really wanted to know, her voice broke as she said, "Ask the Great General about your *abeoji,* not me. I can't answer your questions."

I became afraid, and withdrew into silence.

The cement roads outside Pyongyang and my Pothong River and the red splash of flags had long turned into a stretch of solitary villages and sentry posts, where Mr. Rhee prepared to flash what must have been forged travel documents. He never had to, because of his special license plate. We passed a group of prisoners relieving themselves by the road, mountain after denuded mountain. The countryside frightened me; it always had. The landscape was another country; not my Pyongyang of tree-lined boulevards, a world apart from my youth spent playing sports with the other children at the chandeliered Children's Palace. I tried not to think about my *abeoji,* though my mind was filled with him, or about this man risking his life to save ours. Years later I would hear other stories of people like him.

After a private farewell that I tried painfully to ignore, we got out of the car, and the man spoke to the burly driver of a battered white truck before disappearing into the darkness. It was one of the many private buses that plied the country, one emblazoned with red lines that I would learn was an old Red Cross ambulance. Such symbols meant nothing to me yet. From the back of the truck where only hinges were left of its doors, crouched figures stared out at us. I shrank from their stares, their canvas coats and coarse scarves and, especially, from my growing fear that the differences between us were becoming less important. I'd traveled through the countryside on trips to visit less fortunate relatives, but I hadn't really seen it.

"We're lucky to be here at all." Eomeoni sent me a warning glance from under the scarf and hood veiling her. "Don't forget that."

"Once you wake up, we'll be in China," I whispered to my *dongsaeng,* though saying those words made it too real for me. Smoke exploded from the truck's exhaust pipe, and its engine grunted into the barren rice fields.

"Will we really?" she said, and held on tighter to my hand.

My *dongsaeng* heaved with dry sobs. She had no more tears left—she had wept all night in the security van and the man's sedan that had intercepted it. I kept an arm around her, angry that I could do no more for her. She watched the men who jumped on and off after slipping the driver payments of cigarettes or liquor, and sucked in her breath each time the monotony of the pothole-filled road behind us suddenly revealed a boy shouldering squirming chickens in a sack or women traveling with A-frames on their backs. Shriveled objects in the landscape of harrowed farmland. At each sentry post we flashed our forged papers.

When the truck suddenly lurched and sagged backward to a

stop, the driver got out and slunk over, a cigarette hanging from his lips. "Men push, women out."

It was just a pothole, but my spirits lifted. The organizing, the discarding of my coat, all of me focused on pushing against the hard metal back of the truck. The joints of my fingers popped dangerously, my shoulders made a cracking music, and the fact of the body helped me forget the body.

"A bit of the old back-and-forth," a man said once the truck was on firm ground, and he thrust his hips in and out, laughing with the other older men.

"There are women present," I said, so quietly that no one but my sister could hear.

My sister might have grown into a lovely woman. She might be tall and graceful like my mother but with a sweetness all her own. Even then she was like a deer, quick and easily spooked and so sensitive to others, always knowing when you longed for a book or a Choco Pie and hurrying up to you with her offering. But when Eomeoni handed each of us a sweet potato and said, "I'm so ashamed of myself, but this is all I have to give you for dinner. We need to ration our supply," my sister squeezed her face into a tight ball and refused to accept hers.

Our *eomeoni* turned away. Look at me, her posture said. I've failed as your *eomma*.

She must have felt the failure deeply. She was the kind of *eomma* who stayed up late at night helping us with our projects and skillfully handled a schoolteacher who had slighted my *dongsaeng*. She had no compunction about using bribes and coercion for us, when necessary. Her family mattered most to her. I was angry at her, grateful and confused, and wondered how much I really knew about her. I weighed a sweet potato in each of my hands.

"Eomeoni, sweet potatoes are filling," I said. I would never be able to eat another sweet potato again.

While the driver had a cigarette, I spread a handkerchief across the fender and stripped the skin from both sweet potatoes one long layer at a time.

"Don't you want dinner?" I asked.

My *dongsaeng* shook her head. "I'm so tired and dirty—I can't eat like this." She eyed me cautiously as if expecting punishment. "How can I eat when Abba's nowhere?"

"It's what he would want. If he were here, he would tell you in his politician's voice what it took that farmer to plant that sweet potato."

I conjured up Abeoji on our way to a mountainside holiday, how he would make a curt, careless gesture toward a farming collective. The way his free hand would half-curl as if catching the wind, then open again and release it.

"And he's not nowhere—he's just not here, with us."

"Obba," she said, and started to cry. "You don't have to lie to me and pretend everything's fine. I'm not a baby." She took a sweet potato as if it were a baseball and hurled it into the dark.

A collective gasp roiled from the truck. My *dongsaeng* had never been so fierce or so coarse, and I was paralyzed, unsure whether to be her *obba* and play the disciplinarian or to let her grieve, strike out at the darkness that had swallowed our *abeoji*.

As the sweet potato arced into the dark and became waste, a young *eomma*'s expression brittled with anger. With her baby hanging from a white strip of cloth across her back and neck, she scrambled out and, like a rice farmer, knelt and began hunting. This hunger was everywhere and in the end would belong to all of us, but I only cared about my poor *dongsaeng,* who was hungry for other things.

Eomeoni, who had been shrouded in silence for most of the day, now held my *dongsaeng* tightly to her. She said into the darkness, "Let the farmer keep his sweet potato! My daughter doesn't want your miserable fare."

Night passed into dawn into day then back into darkness. Clouds grouped together, broke apart, formed a claw. Our numbers had dwindled into the group that would cross, and at each checkpoint nearing the border the driver handed out money, alcohol, cigarettes, and packets of powdery *bbindu* to keep the security guards high. All around I saw the broken infrastructure and law of our country; there was nothing that couldn't be bought, evidently, even our safety. All the while our *eomeoni* stayed as still as a frozen movie screen, unapproachable in the folds of her hooded coat.

The *eomma*'s baby began wailing. He opened his tiny mouth and bellowed our misery. My fear was cold and rational. I wanted the baby quiet. I wanted the *eomma* to smother the crying lump of flesh hanging from her neck with the white cloth until it couldn't make another sound, or to feed the baby another sleeping pill. To put to rest those desolate cries that made hope seem impossible. My *dongsaeng* was so tired that she slept through it all. I'm becoming half human, I thought.

"Shut it up or I'll stuff it with rags!" screamed a man.

"Someone will hear us," another said.

Salt filled my mouth. The baby's cries became two slender arms that curled around my lungs, and my breathing slowed and thinned.

Only then did I ask Eomeoni what I couldn't forget, the only question that mattered to me. "I'm his son. I need to know. Tell me: What happened to Abeoji?"

Mr. Choi appeared first as a voice in the dark. The beam of a flashlight aimed toward his own wide, flat nose was the first thing I saw at the border overlooking China. He had us hide from patrolling guards for two nights, waiting for the tightened security to lapse while we rationed our dwindling food supply, until he said it was safe to cross the Tumen River. I would remember the shaved head and the birthmark the shape of a smashed spider across the man's left cheek, though not whether the man had been short or tall. Time has been generous that way, releasing me from one detail, then another.

As we were herded into a van that smelled of timber and wet paper, all I could see was the bullet tunneling into my *abeoji*'s heart.

"They killed your *abba*," Eomeoni had whispered under the truck's rumble, her lips pinched white as she told me what had happened that night. She spoke with her chin resting on the crown of my *dongsaeng*'s sleeping head. "Maybe they would have killed me, too, even if I didn't know anything about his foreign bank accounts. But the Dear Leader considered our good relationship."

I don't know if she told me the truth that night, or her version of the truth, a story more dramatic than the truth. All I have are her words. I wanted to know who was this "they" that my *eomeoni*'s many alliances had saved us from. Who was always this "they"? My head filled with thoughts of Abeoji and the endless tomb of distances between us.

Still, how quickly I got into the van, as if afraid it would leave without me. A boy intent on living even if his *abeoji* was dead.

After we crossed the freezing river and dried off, we were taken by another car to a hut at the edge of a village. My first thought was: Too close. If we sneeze, the villagers will wake up. A car jutted out from the hut's shadow. The blue metal of its door flashed open and a stranger jumped out. He looked at Mr. Choi, then lugged a lumpy sack out of the trunk and dumped out shirts and sweaters that flapped like ghosts in the dirt.

The stranger's red leather jacket made me wary. It didn't look like something a sane man should wear. The man counted us off out loud. Whatever he saw pleased him, for he smiled, flashing a gold filling, and said something in Chinese to Mr. Choi as he withdrew a fat envelope and slapped it into his waiting palm.

"The women first," Red Leather Jacket said in our language this time. "Come on, you want to be buried here? Slower than cattle, these people!"

When my *dongsaeng*'s nails dug into my palm, I said, "This place looks too exposed to be safe."

Red Leather Jacket considered me.

"You're from the south. Pyongyang? You've got the accent, the attitude. Young man, you better learn this quickly: You're in China; now you're nobody."

The man directed the women to take turns climbing through

the break in the wall where they would change into local clothing. We were sent in only after the women reemerged in their new garments. Inside, I tasted dandelions and dried fish and urine in the air. As motes of dust misted down from the roof, I gagged at rats with tails as long as rice stalks rattling in the dark corners.

"Others were here before us," someone said.

In the light shooting through a crack in the roof, I saw plastic bags and empty bottles and flattened squares of straw and tarp for bedding. The hut, filled and emptied many times with the fleeing and the hiding, held the story of our people in its smells. But I didn't think of myself as one of them yet.

I dressed slowly until one by one they left and I was alone again.

"Your first time crossing?" A boy's voice, whistling through a gap between his front teeth, carried in the dark. "You'd do good to stick with me. I know my way around."

The boy I would later call Namil hiccuped and came closer so that I smelled the alcohol on him. I saw his slight silhouette and his smile, so wide it was as if both sides were being pulled apart by strings. He pulled out a bun from his jacket pocket and tore it in half. "Here, you can have some."

"Where did you get this?"

"The trash is high quality here, not like back home. You get fat off what they throw away, really! You'll find out. And the Christians—the good ones—they'll practically give you their house if you look young and sad and tell them you're an orphan."

But I wasn't an orphan. I still had Eomeoni and my *dongsaeng,* one more long journey awaiting us from China to the safety of another country. The boy tucked the piece of bun in my hand though I wasn't going to reduce myself to feeding off garbage. The rats stilled and became attentive. I stared at the stale bread, repulsed, but was touched by his kindness and pretended to take a bite of it.

At a rattling sound outside, the boy instantly turned wary. When a voice spiked in through the crack, he sank behind a couch with filling springing out of its seats. His speed, his animal intuition, made me feel soft, my brain padded by dull fatty layers that didn't know how to read any of the signs around me.

Outside, I saw that Eomeoni had chosen only white clothes, the traditional color of mourning. Her knuckle was locked in her mouth, and I wondered if she was thinking about Abeoji. Or was she crying for our home, our lost lives? Only then I noticed, in the way that time became slow for me, that some men as large as sedans were now positioned behind Red Leather Jacket.

It was as if one of my mother's film reels played in slow motion, the way our men lined up in front of the women. The way some of us were already turned sideways even while standing in front of our women, prepared to run. I stayed behind in the back with my *eomeoni* and my *dongsaeng,* and my hands found theirs without my knowing. A man was shouting, his face inches away from Red Leather Jacket's droopy left eye.

"What are you doing with the baby?" he said.

One of the men trained a gun on him. He stepped back.

They had wrenched the baby from the *eomma,* and the *eomma* had collapsed at Red Leather Jacket's feet, her hands curled around the tops of his shoes. A cry gurgled out of her as he kicked her away from him—I will never forget that sound.

One of the large men turned to Red Leather Jacket. He

pointed at a girl with heavy bangs, at the woman collapsed on the dirt, then at my *eomeoni* and my *dongsaeng*. His associates broke easily through my grip, through the barricade of our men's bodies. Some of us protested as the women were herded to one side, but more quietly now, their minds on the gun.

Nothing was as real as the gun the short squat man pointed at us. Nothing I did could make a difference, but to do nothing was to admit that nothing could be done, and to be alone in the world was to be less than nothing.

All I needed was the gun.

I rushed ahead until my hand brushed against the dull steel. A shoe bore into my spine. Though there was always fighting at school, I had managed to stay beneath the attention of violence, but this time I forced myself up. We struggled, arms confused and tangled with each other. The leaden gun gleamed each time the moon struck it; the man's finger stayed locked into the barrel. How much power was in that hand. It was so close, it was almost mine. But there were too many of them.

Eomeoni screamed as they pinned my arms behind me. The red leather sleeve arced slowly, then it was over. The black butt crunched down on my nose and the burning spread across my face. Coppery blood perfumed the air; I tasted it on my tongue. It will swell, I thought, it will be hard for me to sleep without rolling over, though none of this mattered anymore. Laughter seeped from me at the absurdity and the horror, and I wondered who I would have to become to survive this, until the gun struck down on my nose again.

"You Joseon people," Red Leather Jacket said. "You're too emotional."

The sobbing women were herded past us to a van.

So this was the enemy. The finger curled around the trigger. And this was the enemy: the clouds breaking up, the moon above looming too brightly and exposing us. The blank face of China that made us the hunted. I gazed at the men who were destroying our lives; they looked the same. A swift blur of red leather passed me.

The man opened the back door to the van and invited the women to step up. He looked tired but satisfied that his day was nearly over. Abeoji, Eomeoni, and my *dongsaeng* . . . my mind went silent, into a cool, dark place.

"The women will be taken care of," the man continued. "You do what you're told, then it's not so bad. Some women even like it."

"May I . . . please say good-bye to my son?" Eomeoni spoke quietly, as if not to startle anyone.

"I'm a reasonable person," Red Leather Jacket said, "and you ask like a reasonable woman. Keep it short."

She released my sister's hand. Her loose white pant legs swished as she approached me. I tried to reassure her and tell her, I'll find you, I promise, if it takes my entire life, but my lips wouldn't move. When she took my clammy hands into hers, tears dimmed my sight, turning her features so vague and delicate that I feared I would forget what she looked like.

But I remember so much: her dancer's body leaning into me and her smell of wet pine needles and the promise of spring weather, her gaze that lingered on my face, memorizing. Her bright, fearful eyes as she squeezed my hands and said, "My love, you must be brave."

Part II

The Border

8

Jangmi

In new clothes with a new man and a new name, I thought I could finally leave my country behind and become someone else. I made Seongsik happy. I worked hard to make him happy; I was determined to maintain my devotion until my baby was old enough for us to leave safely. Or maybe we would stay forever with this man, but there was the constant danger of being discovered, and my baby would live as a shadow child who couldn't be registered and officially exist. All through our second week together I made sure that when Seongsik woke up, my soap-scented face was pressed close to his. He craned up to touch me, seeking the son he must have wanted. He would have a baby soon enough. I waited for a safe number of days to pass until I could make my announcement.

Meanwhile, Seongsik followed me to the common room, which was always a remarkable late-spring temperature due to the heated floors, then to the bathroom. When I reemerged, he was waiting by the door to follow me to the kitchen, his movements shy but eager as he walked at my heels. I tried new hairstyles to charm him, laughed helplessly to make him feel more capable. I strived to be a beloved, pleasing wife.

It could have worked. I knew that many women had crossed and married Joseon men for relative safety and given birth to children, and some of them must have escaped capture. Worked, in the only ways that a refugee's life could work. Like those women before me, I was becoming familiar with many things. The camouflage Seongsik's presence gave me in the nearby city's shopping mall, as if I were unafraid of each person who passed us, the smell of pork and beef seeping from everyone's skin. The towers of glistening pastries and watermelons bigger than babies, the soaring plates of food that people in restaurants left half-eaten. Kitchen gadgets that squeezed, ground, separated. So many bewildering freedoms, if you had the money for them.

Memories came back to me, images of my *abba* feeding me what he could find while he starved, my *eomma*'s freckled arms rising up to the sun while she hung the laundry. These thoughts weakened my knees and once forced me to sink to the tile floor, fruit knife still in my hand. My body ached with phantom pain. This, I thought, is what it must be like to lose an arm or a leg.

Still, I felt the eyes on me everywhere. The women on the stairwell when I went to throw out the trash. The building security guard who did nothing but sleep and keep watch, not so different from the guards posted across the river who monitored our villages. In the car on the way to church, Seongsik said, "Stop checking in the mirror. There's no one back there."

But of course there was the security camera at the building's front entrance watching me, a stranger's casual glance. Then there was his daughter.

In those first few weeks in China, Byeol and I had learned that I couldn't eat fish. Or bean sprouts. Or spicy fried tofu. So she demanded that I make these for her every day and made me ache with tension. In front of Seongsik, I feigned having a delicate stomach and counted the days until it was safe to let him know that he had become an *abba*. Would I say it was a premature birth? I decided to worry about that later. The days went by slowly, and as he was often not there, I was left with Byeol and her relentless questions.

"Why can't you eat fish?" or "Why can't you eat bean sprouts?"

"I told you, my stomach is sensitive."

"What is 'sensitive'?" "Why do you like my *abba*?" "Why don't you know how to draw?" "Why can't you speak Chinese?" Then she would look suspiciously at me. One wrong word from a child could get me sent back.

She brightened up each time the doorbell made a rusty ring, which made me freeze, until she remembered that since my arrival she was no longer allowed to answer the door. If her *abba* wasn't home, she would flop in front of the television and prop her chin on her fists and watch cartoons for hours, smiling again.

"Why does the moon change color?" she asked me. "Why do the planets look still when they're supposed to be moving? Why do we have last names? Where is my *eomma*? When is she coming back? Why do boys look so different from girls? Why can't I see God?" Why, why, why? And on and on.

I admired and feared her questions. I wondered if all children were like this.

I patiently answered what I could. But on the evenings when her *abba* was home, she only turned to me and said, "I wasn't asking you. I was asking Abba."

I almost told him in time. I was starting to show despite my mother's genes, but he assumed it was because I often ate three bowls of rice, though I knew that there was always more, and because of my unbearable cravings for the fruit and sweets that were everywhere around me. I ate, then felt overwhelmed by the desire to sleep all day.

"Believe me, there's always more in this country," he would say, laughing, and even I wasn't sure whether it was my greed or my growing baby that drove this hunger.

It happened after he came back from a three-day tour, at dinnertime. I had planned to tell him that night. When my body refused the stew I made with the dried pollack he had brought home, Byeol pointed at me with her spoon and with her mouth full of the *bukeo* stew said, "She doesn't eat fish. It makes her run to the bathroom and throw up."

My throat tightened; he bit into a fresh green pepper dipped in spicy *gochujang,* looking concerned. "Are you sick? When did this happen?"

"From the day after you brought her home." Byeol frowned. "And she doesn't eat bean sprouts or spicy tofu or pickled lotus, either. All of them make her run to the bathroom and throw up. If you have to marry, why don't you marry someone healthy? She's sick all the time!"

She made her best exasperated expression. Seongsik forgot to close his mouth and *gochujang* trickled out and stained his chin a dark red.

I said quickly, "I've never liked fish."

I rested my hand on the bridge of his clenched knuckles and made my first silent prayer: Please let this man weaken at my touch.

He didn't weaken. Instead he stopped speaking to me for the rest of the evening and didn't come to bed. I couldn't sleep. The bed might as well have been made of stone.

Outside, Seongsik and Byeol moved around like red-eyed rats. When I shifted from right to left, the electric blanket beneath me crackled and the blanket above chafed against my skin like pumice. I curled up with dry heaves, but nothing came up, not even my fear. How could I be afraid when I had always taken care of myself with so little help? But I found myself jumping at a branch tapping against the windowpane.

After what felt like hours, Seongsik switched on the light. I shrank from the walls covered with pictures of Byeol, his spiteful face, all of it bathed in an antiseptic yellow.

"You know how much yuan I've spent on you?" He limped to the foot of the bed, his fists positioned on his hips. "Whose baby is it?"

I tried to get up, but he pushed me down by my shoulders. That was what I had become: a woman prostrate before a man. There was no love in his look, no credit earned in the weeks we had spent together. I was owned, and my owner was distraught and capable of punishment.

"I trusted you," he said. I begged him to calm down, but he threw aside the blanket, exposing me.

"It's the past—it has nothing to do with us." I clutched the edge of his trousers. "Please, I'm completely yours."

"You're using me," he said as if he hadn't heard me. He bit down on his knuckles, leaving teeth marks. "All that money and time, and you're going to leave me."

"I won't. You must believe me." I slapped at my forehead. "Where would I go?"

"You're such an actress—you're evil, another Jezebel! A Salome come to see my head on a silver platter!" He shouted insult after insult.

"And what about your past and everything you hid from me?" I felt reckless, myself again, able to finally say something true. "I've been a good woman for you. I've been a good *eomma* to Byeol."

He banged his head against the wall twice, three times, making an angry red dent on his forehead.

"We were supposed to be happy," he said.

How easily the idea of happiness, the possibility of it, slipped from his lips.

"You cost me a lot of money. I had plans for us." His agitated fingers spun through his hair. "You don't deserve to be saved."

"You think you can save me, don't you? You think you're some kind of savior?"

"You're talking back to me? A North Korean woman?"

He punched the heaped-up bedspread with his fists.

"You're going to leave me anyway, so why don't you leave now and wait for the police to do their sweeps? Everyone knows where you people hide—they feel sorry for you, until they don't. Let the police take you to the detention center and send you right back so your government can do what they want to with you, and you know best what they do to an unmarried woman with child. Then you'll wish you had been nicer to me."

I covered my eyes. "Please, just stop."

I was unable to breathe.

He turned to leave. His retreating back, his thin, tuber neck. This man was all I had.

I closed my eyes as one person, opened them as another. Somewhere inside me there was another self hidden from sight. She was watching this other woman pull him to her, gather his chapped brown hands together, and take his index finger between her lips.

"Don't leave me," that other woman said. A thin trail of saliva still connected her lips to him. "Don't leave your wife."

A person can get used to almost anything to survive. That was what China taught me. But I never got used to the fear. The next morning Seongsik claimed that he forgave me and that nothing had changed for us, but that wasn't true. He didn't turn mean, not exactly, but distant, as if I had failed some unspoken test and was no longer worthy of his attention. That day he didn't once step on my heels like a clumsy mutt, and he left the room each time he made a phone call, speaking in a low whisper. At night, he left a wide gap between us on the bed, and forbade me to come any closer. His cold gestures alarmed me, and I began to wake up late at night clawing at the air, trying to escape the truck repatriating

me. I was desperate for him to enforce his rights, make my body laundry scrubbed against a wooden board. I was ready to sacrifice my body to keep my baby safe. My baby.

I was sitting on the floor one morning, a textbook on the Han language spread open on my lap, when Seongsik came in and covered the pages with his hands.

"You're learning Chinese to leave me. You were never planning to stay," he said as if he had just realized this. "That's all you've ever wanted, to get to South Korea."

"No, never. Why would I want something so dangerous?" I tucked my trembling hands between the pages of the book. It was the first time he looked at me directly since he had found out.

"Everyone warned me about trusting a woman from your country. I'm such a *babo*! I never listen."

His words churned deep in my lower stomach and sickness overwhelmed me. The world tipped from one side to another, then righted itself again. I needed Seongsik. But how to convince him that he needed me?

We withered.

"You aren't eating," Seongsik said at breakfast the next day after Byeol had been packed off to school.

I tried to meet his eyes across the bottles of soy and oyster sauce that he had moved into the center of the table.

"Why aren't you eating? It's perfectly good food!" He was so agitated that his words ran into each other.

"I don't feel very hungry." Overwhelmed by the fishy, beany smell, I had pushed the pungent *dwenjang* stew far from me.

I rested my hand on his thigh. He pushed it off and went to the common room.

"You think I'm stupid, don't you?" He pressed his face against the window. "Some kind of bank account to use up?"

I didn't know what a bank account was yet. The loneliness of the new geography, and language, my new body that demanded sleep day and night, overwhelmed me. I began to cry. It wasn't hard to cry as I thought of my baby and how much we needed Seongsik. Need. I wanted to be free from it. The body that demanded food and shelter, that traded safety for sex, how pregnancy weakened it, all of this disgusted me. To be free of your body's needs, I thought, that is true freedom.

He covered his ears with his hands. "Don't cry," he said. "You don't deserve to cry!"

As if someone had pressed a button, my tears stopped. I pressed a cool glass of water across my cheek. "Who's crying?"

He tallied up all my betrayals and pounded his palm with a balled-up fist. When I tried to hold him from behind by the waist and calm him, he threatened to report me to a North Korean official that he said he was secretly friends with. Then he cried and said, "I'm sorry. I'm so sorry."

I was relieved when he left the next morning to guide some Christian tourists. But as the tension stitched into my body began to ease, around noon the doorknob turned and someone called out shrilly, "You! You North Korean girl!"

The voice pricked me. It was his *eomeoni,* who had let herself into the apartment with a spare key. As soon as I greeted her, the doughy-faced woman grabbed me by the hair and yanked me toward the door. The burning went tingling down to my knees, and I just managed to stay on my feet.

"You witch! How dare you stay here!" She let go of my hair. "You don't deserve my son. I'm tempted to call security and ship you straight to a repatriation center."

Terror quickened my heart and a flash of guilt was swallowed up by more terror. How could a woman with child survive alone in this country?

"Eomeoneem." I lowered myself to my knees, enraged and afraid. "Eomeoneem, I have nowhere to go. I'm so sorry. I had no choice."

"Don't soil the word *eomeoni* on your lips. Get work in another city or something, anything." She shivered. "How do you expect my son to look at you anymore?"

"If you want me gone so badly, you could send me to Nam— South Korea." I said it quietly. "I hear they give you resettlement money and I will repay you, I promise. You will be doing a good thing, saving two lives."

That was the wrong thing to say.

She tugged at the front of my shirt with her strong, veiny hands until my shirtsleeve ripped. A button popped off. Her bun came loose and her hair hovered like a thatched roof above her shoulders.

"That's what you always wanted, wasn't it? I won't see my son abused this way."

My hands went to protect my stomach. My ears were ringing when I said, "No, he married me. I'm his wife. The past is the past—I can explain. I had to survive."

"I don't want to hear it! You're not his wife. You're a North Korean, you're nothing."

She pulled her purse open so quickly that she tore the zipper. As my baby moved inside me, I vowed to bear it all and wait until Seongsik returned. He would fix the situation. With time I could make him love me again. I told myself this before she withdrew a handful of yuan and threw it at me.

"Take it before I change my mind."

I tried to follow her into the kitchen, but my legs wouldn't support me. She came back with a bag heavy with what she said was food.

"Take what's here. It's more than you deserve."

"Please, you don't know what I've lost to get here! I'll be a better wife to him than you could ever hope for."

I continued to beg. I considered beating her head in with a heavy pan.

Byeol was at her piano lesson. If she had been at home, maybe she would have pleaded for me, maybe the possibility of yet another new woman in her life would have finally driven her to me. But she wasn't there and I was as alone as ever.

"You forced us to this," she said. "I want you gone before my son gets home. If you don't leave now, I'll call right now and report suspicious behavior in the apartment complex and have you sent back. They don't care, as long as vermin like you are gone. Is that what you want?"

"Think of my innocent baby." I backed up against the book-case. "And your son, your son will get in trouble."

"I am thinking about my poor son." She crossed her arms,

her legs spread out broadly beneath her long skirt. "There are ways. I promise you, there are ways."

What choice did I have? I took what I could carry and left.

I stuck close to the side of the apartment complex, avoiding the eyes of suspicious strangers, passed the towering telephone poles plastered with advertisements. I was no longer anyone's wife, or a North Korean, or a Jangmi. That's what I believed. Only a stranger with a sack of food bulky under her coat.

I walked away from the building. Just then a patrol car pulled into the parking lot and I had a brief view of two men in dark green uniforms before I swiveled back around the side of the building, concealing myself. The cigarettes between their fingers, their relaxed demeanor, made them look so ordinary. That was the way it was with these men who casually destroyed lives after a cigarette.

The time it took to pass the apartment's security camera felt like a crawl. Slow, slow, I told myself. But once my feet were out of the camera's range and far from the officers, I dropped the heavy sack of food and broke into a run. I was terrified and couldn't stop. I slowed only as the fog rolled in. I had never been so unprepared. The fog erased the people, the buildings, erased everything, until I could have been anywhere and anyone. It was the perfect weather for thieves. And lovers.

Under the safety of darkness I found a street of my country's restaurants that Seongsik had pointed out on our first drive in. I saw a few bowls, plates, and chopsticks strewn across green plastic tables in the window of one eatery. The floating islands of leftover noodles and rice they held, all that waste, still shocked me. There were two tin signs, one in Chinese and one in our language, and inside, laminated photos of food were taped to the wall. Its drabness had more in common with my hometown than with the dazzling Chinese cities I had seen on television.

There was also a woman alone. She stretched out her bare feet from under the table and wiggled her fingers in the air with an ease I envied. I pressed close enough that my reflection disappeared. Someday I would be like this woman in her own eatery, surrounded by all that couldn't be taken away. There would be my child beside me in a sunflower print dress, who would never know cold or hunger or suffering. There would be no denouncements, no fear, only my baby girl's feet tapping and the endless sun that would never set. I saw it through the window, the vision that sustained me: my future.

The woman rose and began counting her cash. Her heavier lower half billowed out in a flowery skirt and white pantaloons underneath, and her bucolic shuffle contrasted with the industry of her quick hands. She reminded me of my mother.

I entered into the amber light.

"Please."

I gestured at the bowl of half-eaten noodles on one of the creaky plastic tables. I wanted to save Seongsik's mother's money, the little I had.

"I just want something—anything—to eat and then I'll go."

The woman's eyes met mine and became unfriendly. "You're

from across the river?" she said. Whatever kindness in her was gone.

"What you have left over, anything."

"You people," the woman said, and again I was struck by the feeling that I was no longer a person, but one of many, to her. "After you beg for free food and clothes, you're always coming over and stealing eggs and rice from the same people who helped you. A whole cow disappeared in the next town. And now you want my noodles."

I gazed beyond the woman's shoulder to the bowl. "But I'm not like that. The food will go to waste anyway, so I thought—"

"They say an old granny was killed by one of you. She was always helping your kind, then one of those she'd helped robbed her and took everything she had in the house, which wasn't much."

I hadn't robbed or stolen from these people; I was sure I could never kill anyone. "Even the broth—that's all I need. That's all my baby needs."

The woman picked up a bowl of leftovers from the table. My hands were outstretched and waiting when cold noodles hit my face.

"Not for your kind." The woman wiped her hands on her apron. "I've had enough of you. Get out before I report you and they haul you back to where you came from."

9

Danny

The border between the two countries was long, and on the winding road heading south for the random town I'd settled on, all I saw from the bus were the mountains veiny with snow. In fact, there was nothing left to distract me from my fear. I'd turned off my cell phone from the outset. The idea of my mom with another man made me shiver with shame, and I didn't know what to tell my dad. Returning home meant facing school and Adam, but going back to my mom's wasn't an option, either. I wondered why God was testing me.

I arrived at dusk, the Tumen River as thick as a blanket in front of me. The lights in the storefront windows of the town went out like dominoes in slow motion; the lights of cubicle-size residences lit up one by one. I stared up at those low-rise apartments, convinced that no one could possibly be as unhappy as I was. I wandered aimlessly with my backpack, the hallway lights tattooed across my mom's face in my mind.

By late evening I knew too well the dusty stores along the main

strip with dusty products and the ubiquitous red neon signs adver-
tising everything from adult entertainment to car parts. I wore layers of new clothes I'd bought from a local store to disguise myself
and kept a cap low over my face and ducked away anytime I saw
someone who looked remotely like my mom. When a bundled
homeless granddad rattled a can in my face, I told him, "No, I'm
like you," and the man shot me a venomous look as if he were
deeply insulted. I tried to check into a run-down motel, but the
manager insisted on taking down my identification card or passport number as was the law, which would help my mom track me
down and lasso me in. I checked into a bathhouse instead. Only
then I finally gathered the courage to call my dad.

I lay down across the common room's heated floor in the corner, flipped open my cell phone, and used my phone card to call
home. On the second ring, my dad picked up.

"Daehan? Where are you? Your poor *eomma* is nearly dead
from worry. Do you have any idea what you've done to her? I
was about to fly out and look for you."

"Dead from worry? She's perfectly fine. Believe me, she's more
than fine."

As I realized all that I could never tell him, I felt the distance
between my dad and me growing into a big fat canyon.

"I'm fine, too. I'm just checking in so you won't worry about me."

"Go back to your *eomma* now, wherever you are. We just
want you home."

"I'd rather stay where I am. I need time."

"Time for what? Did something happen?"

"Dad, I need time on my own to figure things out."

"None of this would have happened if your *eomma* hadn't suddenly changed phones without telling me. She never tells me anything. Don't do anything to yourself, please! Daehan, for us!"

"Dad, I promise I won't do anything stupid. Double promise, in front of God. I just need time."

He didn't understand. "Don't do this to us. You're a good boy; there's nothing to figure out. You need to come home."

I apologized and apologized, then hung up.

I wanted to be far away from my parents and from everything that had happened. To know that I was capable of surviving on the streets because I was one hundred percent masculine. That was probably mainly behind my move to the streets a few nights later, though I told myself it was to save my yuan for emergencies. It was as if I was onstage and Adam and his friends, the kids at Bible camp, were my audience.

After walking through the whole town I took up residence in a half-abandoned building made of cubicles of shops. I used my canteen to sprinkle water on the floor and wiped it down with toilet paper, stacked up my worldly goods, and pondered what God was trying to tell me.

I was shaken awake and blinded by a flashlight. I scrambled up, wishing I had my slingshot and marble in hand and ready to shoot, until I saw they were kids around my age. I became excited; I was lonely for people. But these guys had mean looks.

One with Chinese characters tattooed down his wrist spelling out "Of the Universe" said, "Don't you see the lines drawn showing what's ours and what's yours?"

"Lines, what lines?" I strained my eyes at the floor.

A stocky kid pushed me down to the slab of cement. "Still can't see it? The line I'm about to make on your face." He told me to leave.

"There are so many other rooms," I said. He didn't look convinced. "I'll just move to another room."

"Every one of those rooms are ours." He spat on my foot. "This is our territory."

I was groggy, frightened, and my thoughts returned to my mom's apartment, a place I finally decided was worse than the cold and the grime. After much searching, I found an apartment building complex at the edge of town left in mid-construction, as if the developer realized that there would be no buyers around by the time it was finished. Rusted wires poking up as high as bamboo shoots from the cement floor and the concrete pillars made it a pretty bleak obstacle course. Lying down, I saw sleeping pigeons above me roosting on the skeletal roof.

I prayed daily and tried not to lose my way. I washed in the public bathroom and reminded myself, as I stepped around puddles of urine, that at least I wasn't in high school. I approached restaurants and collected the day's leftovers in exchange for running errands. Hurt and anger rattled in my head like loose marbles, so I disciplined myself with a regimen of push-ups. I willed the asphalt into packed dirt, the town into a state park, the food scavenging into foraging in the forest, reimagining this as a familiar Boy Scouts trip. I added details to my map of the town in my notebook. Maps help you find your way and guarantee that if you're careful you won't stray off course. I was sure that with a map I could avoid future suffering.

The next week I began collecting cardboard for a few coins from the recycling center, but during a bathroom break someone stole the entire day's stack from me, along with my precious parachute cord, the most durable of ropes. I reminded myself that though Job had been enslaved for seven years I'd had less than two weeks of setbacks. I found work in an eatery instead, where the severe thin-lipped lady complimented me on my system of washing and stacking. My diet improved dramatically. At night I set the alarm on my watch for an early wake-up, which reminded me to call my dad the next day. I tried not to think about my mom.

I was lonely. A few weeks passed with only the sour-faced owner of the eatery for company. She liked how I worked but more than once said, "You talk more in an hour than I do in a week." I can't pretend I didn't think of home.

At night I reread the same two books: *Three Kingdoms* and a book on *baduk*-playing strategies. I became a fountain of speech for myself, a delirium of quotations and epiphanies. I talked to God. I began to hear God everywhere: in honking cars, the beating of pigeon wings, a water fountain's bubbling, the *whoosh!* of a school swing. He was north, south, east, and west for me. He was the boy peeing against a wall, the umbrella pines fanning mightily in a private conversation, and I was the sky and the earth and they were me, and the night wasn't so scary anymore once the roofless building filled with the Word, the Word being God. One night, in that deep peace I would never feel again, I heard footsteps.

I thought, finally, I was meeting God.

Before I saw the man, I saw his feet. His black shoes, laced so tightly they looked as if they were about to snap, stepped through the hole that was my door. Next his black suit that made him look like a typical gray-haired businessman, then his round face as serious as the Bible and so unlined that he must have never smiled or frowned. He walked steadily, even with the rusted wires shooting up from the floor, as if he was the kind of man for whom there were no obstacles, only a destination.

"Is anyone there?" he called out in Korean.

I recalled my mother's warnings about organ thieves thirsty for my juicy liver or kidneys and Chinese mafia that carved out a person's lungs for the fun of it. He might be a Joseon-*jok* like me, maybe one who sold boys into some seedy industry. I scrambled to get away, but my leg caught in my plastic wrap. His eyes focused on me as I heaved up again, praying for the superhuman strength of action-movie heroes, but I fell forward, more Marx Brothers than Superman. I probably would've broken my nose and more if the man hadn't caught me in his arms. He did so gingerly, as if he disliked intimacy.

I flung myself backward and in a flash I had my slingshot and polished stones ready.

"Don't be afraid," he said. "I'm not a bad person."

I kept quiet. He pulled away the rest of the plastic until it surrounded me like wilted flower petals, and I was inches away from his pencil-sharpened eyebrows. His hair, his pupils, and the shadow above his lips were the color of ash. His eyes flashed across me while I considered whether it was sinful to slam him in the groin and run. He looked puzzled, and disappointed, and he repeated what he had just said in Chinese.

That I couldn't abide. I didn't appreciate being mistaken for one of the Han people, and told him as much in Korean.

"A Joseon-*jok*." He said it in Korean this time. "What are you doing here, then? Where are your parents? I could've been someone you wouldn't want to see."

"I don't know where my parents are." I didn't see it as a lie, not exactly. Burdened with a distant father and a mother who had gutted the core of the seventh commandment, I viewed myself as a kind of Christian orphan.

His bland expression softened. "My own parents were killed by the Japanese in the war. I was young, too, but the church took care of me. You shouldn't be out alone like this. There are organizations for orphans and other kids like you."

I was pretty sure that those organizations would lead me right back to the deacon and my mom.

"I don't like institutions."

He sighed. "Many of you don't. You don't live here like this all the time, do you? You'll get pneumonia."

I said nothing.

He assessed my clothes, my bag, the corner I had scouted for myself. He put his hands together as if in prayer.

"All Christians are friends," he said.

I reached up for the cross that was now protruding over my shirt collar.

"Can I bring you food, a blanket? Help you in any way?"

"I have friends. They're coming for me."

He had an impassive face, like a rocky cliff, and I could only guess at his intentions until he drew out a piece of paper and scrawled a basic map and the name of a restaurant on it.

"I often eat here," he said. "She's a good woman. Whenever you need something—anything—ask for me. You can call me Kwon *ajeoshi*."

That early spring evening as I was leaving work, two men pulled me into the shadows of an alley. I tried to break away, but they slammed me against the brick wall. It happened so quickly that the shock only hit me when an arm jabbed into my chest.

"Hand over your bag," said the man with a bald spot exposed like a medieval tonsure. He was a Han Chinese and blew out cold puffs of air as he spoke.

"Here's my wallet and my watch." I offered up my wrist. My passport, which I considered my life, was tucked into the bag's deepest compartment.

"I said your bag." The man straightened, his voice louder. "You think I'm asking?"

I fumbled with the backpack, but I finally managed to get it open. "You'll see that most of what's in there is of no value to anyone but me."

"You think I'm joking, kid?"

I shook my head.

That was when the tonsured man flipped open a jackknife and twirled it until it sliced through the air and rested against my Adam's apple. Within seconds, the two of them stripped me of my possessions, taking even my waterproof boots. The knife stayed by my neck, and it sparked the same strong desire to live that I'd felt when I'd nearly drowned. I was fearful, my heart and head racing at the prick of the cold blade, when the sound of glass cracked behind me and someone shouted in warning. The criminals turned and ran deep into the alley.

Apparently I had been rescued. I slumped against the wall, weak and grateful and ashamed. Rescue reminded me of desperate maidens stuck in towers and sleeping beauties stretched out on beds of vermilion roses, waiting for their prince. Nothing made me more uncomfortable. I wanted to be the kind who did the rescuing.

I was also strangely at ease. The tall one with grave looks and a pensive droop to the corners of his eyes approached me under the streetlight, calming the breakneck speed of my heart. He shouldn't have; he was clenching the neck of a soda bottle, an image incongruous with his fair, Asian pear skin and out-of-focus features. I had never seen such a beautiful man. He set the bottle down before facing me.

"Are you all right?" he said with such concern that I pretended that I was better than I felt.

"They took my bag, they took everything."

I had lost my passport, my identification cards, my tools, everything except the cash tucked into my underwear and the inner lining of my pants. Daniel Daehan Lee, a citizen of the People's Republic of China and a permanent resident of the United States of America, was now paperless, undocumented, as if I had never existed. I rubbed where the cold knife had pressed against my skin, feeling strangely free.

"Look, *hyeong,* they even took his shoes," said the other, much smaller kid, sounding impressed. His cap was pulled down low over his face, and his voice crackled with the same awkward change I had suffered a few years ago.

The young man I'd call Yongju considered me, then told me to lift up my foot. I did as he said. He ripped his scarf in half with one great pelican motion of his long arms, then wrapped the two halves around my feet.

I didn't know what to say. It was April and still chilly, and it was clear from their straggly hair and pants stiff with dried mud that they didn't have many choices, though maybe I didn't look so different from them by then. Yongju's slender neck was now exposed. And still he had given me his scarf, he had risked himself for a stranger.

"That'll do for now," he said. "You'll have to find a pair—"

"Or steal one later," said the smaller kid.

We mutually assessed the situation. The soft modulation of Yongju's voice and the draping of his hands made me long for those mysterious friendships that I'd watched from the sidelines back in America.

"You have anywhere to go?" Yongju finally asked.

"Not really." I found myself whispering though the city had long shut down, and at its fringes, where we were, there was no one else in sight.

"You wouldn't like where we are." He jerked his head toward the mountains. "It's primitive. And far."

"You're a Joseon-*jok,* aren't you?" The smaller one I'd learn was Cheolmin lifted up his cap to have a closer look at me. I saw that part of his forehead and cheeks had been burned, giving his skin an uneven, blistered texture. His inflamed gums showed when he smiled.

"My name's Daehan," I offered. "Yeah, I'm a Joseon-*jok.*"

"The burn happened at a lumber mill in your country," said Yongju. I'd been caught staring at Cheolmin's face.

Cheolmin said, "Maybe Joseon-*jok.* Or he could be a spy from down South."

Yongju made a small noise, something between a quiet chuckle and a sigh. "Our country's in bad shape, but not that bad. You think anyone can be a spy?"

I said, "I know how to start fires from practically nothing, I can build huts and know the difference between good and bad mushrooms. And I'm practically a compass. And there're lots of other things I know how to do. I'm pretty useful." I stopped, surprised by myself.

"*Meojori,* that's a big mouthful of bragging about yourself," said Cheolmin, frowning.

I didn't know what *meojori* meant, but it didn't sound pleasant. The modus operandi in East Asian cultures was modesty, but I've never gotten the game of humility right, or its opposite, what I call the American swagger. I tried correcting myself. "I'm just trying to say . . . I wouldn't be an absolutely terrible burden to have around."

Though our accents were more or less the same, by then it was clear to me that these two were not Joseon-*jok.* For one, there was their peculiar diction. And from the onset Yongju was too vigilant and tense, making broad sweeps of the scene with his eyes.

Cheolmin was no different, his neck jerking to look behind him like a tic, his hands flexing and bunching together with his breath.

"Come on, we have to keep moving," Yongju said.

He retreated from the alley. Cheolmin followed, a sour smell trailing behind him. No one outside my family had ever put themselves on the line for me; I wasn't about to let them walk away. When we turned the corner I found my plastic cover that the crooks had tossed, ignorant of its usefulness even with a hole in it, and my books. No one ever seemed to want books. I dusted them off.

The two moved steadily toward the mountains. I continued following them.

Cheolmin lurched at me, his fist raised in the air. "There's no space for you!"

I halted midstep.

Yongju said, "There could be space. You heard what Namil said last night, it would help to have a Joseon-*jok* with us." He turned to me. "You'd be a good scout?"

"How can we trust him?"

"My *eomma* was born across the river in Hamgyong-do, actually. We crossed back into China early."

"Really? Your *eomma* was from our country?"

Cheolmin looked suspiciously at my clothes.

"That must've been really early. You've got Chinese papers, I.D. card, everything?"

"I did, but . . ." I waved my hand at the alley that was no longer behind us. I didn't mention my next crossing to America—

considering what America meant to their country, I assumed they wouldn't accept me if they knew.

Yongju said to Cheolmin, "You know a group's the only way you survive, Joseon-*jok* or not. His kind can help out—they can scout ahead and approach people without any danger. Let's take him with us."

"It'll be crowded, *meojori*." Cheolmin spat as he cursed but began walking anyway.

"Come on."

Yongju rested a hand on my shoulder.

"Come with us."

10

Yongju

This was my China: a mountain dugout opening into a cave several meters deep. The drip of water during rain, the scratchy music of the trees outside. A bed of stones and paper to keep the cave dry. Blankets, clothes from the city dump, and donation bins we would break into, anything to create heat in the chilly underground. A small cry, a young, pebbly voice floating alone in the dark, then silence.

Each morning I woke up in the hollow full of orphans who had crossed out of hunger, to the music of misery in their arrhythmic breathing, the grinding of their rotten teeth. The morning cold burrowed into my bones and made its home there and my hands and knees became slippery on the cool earth, and my eyelashes thick with the loose soil that trickled down. It was so dark that the word *dark* was inadequate. So dark it was as if I was dead. The cave was full of haunted life and the stink of urine, and the only relief was to close my eyes and pretend that the darkness wasn't there.

When the truck drove away with our women, I had collapsed into the beveled tire tracks, stared down at my useless hands, and searched for words to comprehend how I felt. Grief. Wretchedness. Disbelief. But there were no perfect words. The men left behind began to talk. There was some heated discussion between us, a little pushing.

Someone said, "We're too close to the border. This place is crawling with surveillance."

Another said, "We have to make our own way."

One man gripped his chest as if to hold his heart in.

Soon they scattered under night's sheath. Some must have headed for the mountain ranges nearby; the bold or lazy ones followed the winding paved road or looked for a sympathetic farmer who might hire them and give them a corner to sleep in. Maybe a few had relatives, a phone number, a lead. It didn't matter to me then. All I could do was stare. Sound subsided. I sat crouched for so long that matter melted and my legs grew roots into the dry packed ground. I became the trunk of a tree. I no longer felt cold, heat, sadness, or fear.

Maybe I would have lapsed into sleep and frozen that night and died peacefully. But something moved in the periphery of my sight.

I ripped a branch off a rotting tree and clutched it between us. Splinters embedded in my palms, but I didn't feel them until later.

It was the boy from the hut. He said, "I'm on your side! It's me! Remember, the bun?"

I saw the outlines of his face in the dark, then the black gaps between his teeth.

He jumped up and down, warming himself up. "It's your first time crossing, isn't it?"

I nodded.

"You came alone? With parents?"

I shook my head. "I'm alone now."

When he saw that I wasn't going to move, he said, "You can't stay here. You want to get as far away from the border as you can, and you better learn the Han people's language. Fast. The *ganna saekki* get everyone by the border, just wait. It's my third time crossing. The first time I got picked up the morning after I crossed. They'll send you back into the asshole of our country—you're older than me, and you don't want to know what they'll do to you."

I didn't care. I sank my head into my hands and stayed huddled. But Namil waited for me.

The cave took us hours to reach. Namil said the group he'd stuck with when he crossed the last time had discovered it by following an older man. The man had left, vowing to walk all the way to a safe country if he had to.

At first I didn't leave the cave. But I quickly realized that I needed to do my share and help the others, who spent their time in a hopeless cycle of collecting wood or working at small farmsteads or at logging sites that dotted the mountains for food with no pay. I cleaned myself as best I could, hoping that my height differentiated me from the other four boys, who were stunted in growth by their lean years of living. I began venturing out to the nearest town in search of work, food. Information. I was afraid of every single person I met, knowing what it would mean to be repatriated. Shadows scared me. A stranger's voice, footsteps, all of it sent me on dizzying detours. I had never been so afraid of people.

I forced myself to burrow through the nearest village dump to salvage what we could use. Sometimes I found canned goods. What people discarded in China amazed even me. I rinsed out a pigpen in exchange for eggs and potatoes, and back on the mountain I planted my first potato eyes. We rotated all-night guard duty in case our cave, which we had camouflaged with tin and brittle branches, was raided. I slept with my shoes on.

Once I was beaten by an old farmer for no reason, except that he could. I was no longer a privileged Pyongyang man but a North Korean that you could abuse without punishment, and the locals knew it. I learned that a North Korean man in China was less than a man, less than the dogs or cats that every Han Chinese person seemed to raise. You could be murdered for working too slowly. Entire villages of our women were said to be held captive, slaves in bed and in the field, which made me think of my *eomma* and *dongsaeng*. Some of our people who I briefly met had lived in hiding for years. I had never thought of myself as an angry person, but I was getting angrier. I lived inside the mouth of a giant beast, and that beast was China.

Hope was a distant island. The other boys only aspired to be like ghosts, invisible, and thought about how to get food and smoke and drink. They lived in the present tense, too afraid to desire more. But Daehan was different; he was educated and spoke in the future tense, and he gave me back a little hope.

"You want to see something?" Cheolmin said to Daehan.

He had ignored Daehan all week, like the others, but tonight Daehan had brought leftover meat from a town market over two hours' walk away and started a small fire the size of a pear blossom for grilling. He trudged into town and coaxed vegetables to grow in the stubborn mountain soil, laboring at any job he could. As a Joseon-*jok,* he was safe from everything, it seemed, but loneliness.

"Don't let him show you," said Gwangsu, who was a mere baby when his *abeoji* was taken away, maybe to the camps or to jail, for stealing food. His *eomma* had been seized after they crossed into China.

"Keep your mouth shut, *saekki-ya,*" said Cheolmin.

With a ballerina's agility, Cheolmin leaned against a tree and pulled off a shoe a few sizes too large and two pairs of socks. He braced his foot up high so close to Daehan's face that even in the dark, he must have seen that it was blackened with frostbite.

Daehan studied the foot respectfully. "That's rough. How did it happen?"

Cheolmin told the same story he recounted each time he got drunk, but with every telling the number of guards at the river, the water's depth and temperature as his foot broke through the ice, changed. I had told them very little, holding that terrible night close to me, though the others already knew about me because of Namil.

I said, "We have to leave. And we will. Someday it will happen."

Cheolmin, the angriest, most unpredictable of us, poked Bakjun in the side. "You know what our *dongmu* from the great city of Pyongyang keeps saying? He says he's going to find his *eomma* and *dongsaeng*. How're you going to do that in China? This country's as big as Mars!"

"You can't talk to him like that. He's older than you! Don't you have any respect for your *hyeong*?" said Daehan, when it was obvious that Cheolmin didn't. He added, "If he says he's going to find them, he's going to find them."

The next day, in the stubborn, practical manner I would come to associate with Daehan, he thrust at me a written list of possible steps to take, some that I hadn't thought of and others that I wouldn't dare attempt. He trailed after me when I went twig hunting and silently watched me kick the face of a granite rock slope until I was too tired to go on. We said nothing to each other and in the easy silence walked back together.

A week later he said, "Why don't we walk to the nearest city? I know it's a long way, but there's supposed to be a church there."

"A church?"

"That's where Christians gather."

"Christians? Those South Koreans that the boys say are generous with handouts?"

"They're not always South Koreans, and they're far more than an easy handout."

From his lengthy monologue, I gathered that these Christians could help our people reach a safe country. I hadn't known that churches were illegal in China and most Christians clustered underground in house churches; I hadn't known much. The Chinese border of the Joseon-speaking people was an exception. Contact with Christians could mean death if I was caught by the police and repatriated, since my country feared Christianity, he said, so I could wait nearby while he met the pastor in charge.

The next day, as the night became a vein of light rimming the horizon, we washed at the nearest icy brook the best we could and made the four-hour walk into the city together. He rambled on, as was his habit, through the valleys of bare trees and narrow dirt roads while circumventing the villages of mud huts and small towns. I didn't mind. I was a quiet person and liked to listen.

"Did I tell you about," he would begin, and I would learn many things, interesting things, about animals I'd never seen such as orcas and emperor penguins, and robots that defeated any man at *baduk*. He was an educated Joseon-*jok* with more of a future than us, but in his rare pauses his smile turned south, as if his bright energy were a vast production of effort made to convince himself.

As we passed in the distance a farmer working in a cornfield, Daehan said, "You have a *hyeong,* too?"

"No." I swallowed. "Only the *dongsaeng* you already know about."

I was grateful when he pressed no further.

The crisp air and sunlight flushed through us, then the city was upon us. We walked in silence as the huts turned into towering apartments and the yeasty smell of a beer factory. There were so many cars that I was afraid to cross the street, afraid of being recognized as North Korean. Numbness spread from my heart to my hands as the words *dongsaeng, eomeoni, abeoji* rang in my ears like restless bells. Maybe it was the same for Daehan, for he had become quiet.

When Daehan saw me hold back, he said briskly, "Follow me!"

He crossed the street at an even, steady pace with the cars.

"Look at the budding trees!"

He was himself again, pointing out the cloudless sky, the swinging pigtails of two girls in an apartment's playground, his words fleeing darker subjects. Brown hills rose from behind brown apartments, and magpies scattered as we passed.

"Straighten up and look like you belong here," Daehan said.

I realized I was hunching, trying to make myself invisible.

"With your height it's not hard."

I said, "You're different from the other Joseon-*jok* kids on the streets."

He looked at me. "You must feel a whole world between you and the others—it's like putting a beluga whale in with a group of panthers."

"Why do you stay? I can't help wondering. You're too educated and you have other options."

He looked wounded. "You mean you don't want me here?" His hands mined down deep into his pockets.

It was as I had suspected. He needed people, and for reasons known only to him, he had no one.

The redbrick church looked like a giant eye, a tower of sight. As we stood looking at it from across the street, I waited for Daehan to lead us.

"Not to worry." He patted my arm as if he were the older one. "I was practically raised in the church. You'll be safe here."

"Let's go, then." I was grateful for his confidence, his vocabulary of hope.

Daehan's overgrown hair curled up at his collar, his skin was brown and flaky, and his black clothes a shade of gray despite our morning wash, but he strode inside as if he were entering his own house.

I took one step forward, then another, and was blinded. Searchlights, spotlights, but it was only the sun beaming down through a skylight. The building was plain inside, and a painting of a bearded man hung on the wall.

Daehan pointed to it. "That's Jesus, God's son."

What he said meant nothing to me. Still, the church was beautiful: Sunlight soared in through the high windows and cast its warm spell over the burnt-honey varnish of the long seats he called pews. I passed a large wooden cross hovering over the podium, seemingly midair.

Daehan skidded down the empty aisles and approached the doors at both sides of the central platform. I followed. I was suddenly terrified. There could be a security patrol lying in wait behind the doors, or even the Dear Leader himself, though that was absurd.

"Is anyone there?" He tried the door to the left.

I was ready to flee when the door opened, Daehan jumped back, and a stooped man with a thick rug of hair ambled out.

He looked us over. It didn't matter that I had tried to wash in the icy stream or clean my wool coat and trousers; my new life must have marked me like a prison uniform.

The man said, "What can I do for you?"

Daehan propelled himself forward.

"We're looking for the leadership of this church. The pastor, preferably." He sounded polite and educated.

The man said he was the pastor and that we had caught him just in time; he was on his way out. His eyes were wide and frank, and I had no choice but to trust him.

Daehan spoke rapidly, braiding together words so foreign that at first I wondered if it was a Korean dialect. Only much later did I understand that he was trying to gain the pastor's trust with his Christian credentials.

I couldn't wait. "I heard that you help . . . people."

The man smiled, but the language of his body turned wary. His eyes, perfectly shaped black stones, stayed trained on me.

As if he were afraid we would be seen, he quickly led us into the back to his office. Twenty young men could have slept in his office. I was starting to measure space by the number of people it could hide. The pastor's books had outgrown their shelves and littered the room's available surfaces. Across his desk were scattered a collection of pens and files piled like felled logs.

The pastor pushed his eyeglasses up the bulbous slope of his nose and looked kindly at me. "Why don't you tell me about yourself?"

Daehan studied the bookshelves and pretended not to listen. For the first time I tried to form a coherent narrative of who I was, where I came from, and what had happened to my family. It embarrassed me to talk about myself at such length, and my speech circled back on itself as I wondered if this was how it had actually happened and, especially, how much to reveal, whether I should change dates and places to protect myself. The discomfort of I, I, I. It struck me that, for the pastor, the most important thing about me was that I was North Korean.

He listened patiently, his large head bobbing to indicate he understood. After I stopped speaking, he said to Daehan, "Was this your idea?" He said it as if he meant: What do you want from me?

Daehan's lower lip jutted out in a dogged way. "My *eomma* always taught me the church was for the poor and needy."

The pastor thought for a moment, then asked us to wait. "I have something for you."

When he returned, he looked serious and sad, as if my weight had become his, and I felt hopeful that this man could help me. He set a plastic bag down on the floor between us.

"Son, I think these will fit."

They were clean clothes, including a worn, padded coat. He patted me awkwardly on the shoulder, then handed me a few boxes of rice cakes and an envelope. Money, I guessed, from the envelope's feathery heft.

"We collect regular donations for the North Koreans who come to us for help. Many donate, the community, guests, South Korean groups. This should aid you a little."

But I didn't want supplies to sustain me for another mere week or two.

"I need help. I need to find my family." I clutched his hands. When he tried to pull away, I didn't let go.

"I've been told that Christians are good people." I looked into his eyes. "You must know what it's like for me. I have lost everyone I love. Everything was a lie, and everything here is new and foreign. I'm a university student surrounded by crass, ignorant *kkotjaebi* from our country—we don't have a single cell in common. Imagine waking up to rats and eating food out of the garbage. All I'm capable of here is enduring each day, but it isn't enough to endure. If you help me to South Korea, there are things I can do there, good things, and I promise you that I will—I will—" I couldn't finish.

"Please, child, don't cry." He offered me a clean handkerchief.

"Please." I began lowering myself to my knees, but Daehan forced himself between us and stopped me.

"The answer's self-evident," said Daehan. "The only moral thing to do is to help him escape out of China."

"You think it's that easy?" The pastor looked enraged, then discouraged. "When I was a university student, I used most of my modest funds to shelter and feed the first famine victims crossing the river. That was in the nineties, when the hunger was at its worst."

His eyes became sad and were no longer focused on me. I realized that I was just one of the thousands who had come to him since with swollen abscesses and scabby skin, clutching his hands the way I had held his.

"My children, there have been massive crackdowns since then, you see."

One hand rubbed at his temple and he kept his chin angled to the ground.

"We are here to preach and spread the word of God to the Han people, but if we help a North Korean, we're expelled or, worse, the church is shut down, and all this effort, our life's work, comes to an end. Many, many people are terribly hurt as a result. God is with you, my child, but for the sake of the church, it's dangerous for me to be here with you like this. I'm afraid there's nothing more I can do for you. You see, there are too many of you now."

In an eatery I forced down an octopus ball with a second bottle of *baiju*. Why not? There were only four hours of walking ahead of us. I felt reckless, and wanted to be drunker than I had ever been.

Daehan tried to steal my bottle away. "It's an ideal time to go back home, don't you think? You realize this isn't very discreet."

I was so drunk, I walked through a crowd without fear for the first time. Rage churned in my gut.

Still, I wasn't drunk enough not to be afraid when an official-looking truck passed us and turned at the next corner. The kind of truck that might gather up our people and force us back across the river. The smoky octopus came up and invaded my lungs, and Daehan followed me as I fled the city, my hand tight around the plastic case in my pocket that held a razor blade, the one I had crossed the river with to use in case we were caught. I still had choices.

When we reached a one-lane country road, it began to rain. We walked past houses sprinkled across the unfriendly land like an afterthought.

Daehan was mostly quiet, but suddenly he said, "It must be freeing to be old. You know, to be so old someday that you're too exhausted to feel. To be without dreams."

"You talk about age," I said. "In our country most people are young and without dreams."

I looked at the peaks ahead and felt the long night descend. There were rumors that one of our people had walked down the paved road right into a patrol, giving them no choice but to arrest him. Poor, foolish man, the words came with each thundering beat in my head, and I wondered out loud what might happen if I walked blindly, right now, to the country that Daehan called South Korea, our Nam Joseon.

"You know that's suicide," Daehan said fiercely. "Don't give up."

"After I crossed, I learned that the stars in the sky are mere pictures. Something like that."

"You mean they're real?"

He stopped laughing after I heaved up my food, the sea scent of octopus scorching my tongue. He forced me to continue.

When he spotted a hut inside the fold of mountains, we made a long arc around it. People were dangerous, and their grunting, barking animals more dangerous still. Brambles grabbed at my pants. The mountain was alive. The roots of its trees seemed to rise and snarl my feet and trip me. Mud sucked at my shoes and I sank into the mountain's flesh. I would have lost my will, and my way, if it weren't for Daehan.

The rain stopped, but the moon and the stars were hooded by clouds and were useless guides. I scrambled in the dark behind Daehan, who took to the mountain slope the way I imagined a goat would. My hand groped around a prickly tree, then around boulders. I was so tired; I wanted to rest on the wild grass. It was soft under my hand, beaten down by the rain into a pillow.

The wind carried the smell of wilderness. I looked around; the musky smell was too close. The undergrowth of the bushes' dark outlines rustled, was set quivering, and then I saw it: the bristly shadow, a pair of eyes glowing faintly out at us.

"What's that?" I whispered.

"I don't know," Daehan whispered back.

I lowered myself, kept to the ground. Maybe it was a squirrel or a rat. Please let it be a rat. But the eyes were too high up. A deer? It was large and seemed to grow larger in front of me, as if it wasn't an animal at all but some monstrous creature come to track me down. I waited, alert with fear, watching it watch me. But when the clouds blew in another direction and the moon was bright again, Daehan clapped his hands.

"No, no, it's a woman," he said. "A pregnant woman, I think, from the silhouette."

I saw her for the first time. Jangmi, her eyes wide and bright with fear.

11

Danny

That April I woke up each morning in the cave as dark as a mother's womb. It was damp and smelled worse than a gym locker room, but the choir of breathing tickling my ears was reassuring. When I shifted, my back scraped against layers of stones and paper and my tarp, which I'd laid underneath us to keep the moisture out. The warm bundle beside me moved, too. It was Yongju. I made sure it was always Yongju beside me.

Everything changed when Jangmi came. The next morning, when I wiggled out from under the filthy blankets, there was a gap beside me where Yongju should have been. I crawled toward the morning light, one hand out in front as I tried not to wake anyone up. Outside I saw what I'd feared.

Jangmi was sitting on a boulder, her hands folded over her swollen belly as Yongju dusted off dirt and silvery threads of cobwebs from her hair. They looked as if they'd been up and talking for hours. He gently pulled her hair back into a loose knot as if to see better her heart-shaped face and skin carved out of a perfect piece of marble. She clearly spelled trouble, and I found myself praying that he was only giving her hair a final cleaning. He murmured something and she looked like a queen speaking to her audience when she responded. That was when I squeezed in between them and slung my arm around Yongju's shoulders.

I said, "What are you two doing up?"

Yongju flushed as if I'd caught him kissing her.

"What are *you* doing here in the mountains with us?" she said, though the sweetness of her voice reminded me of blooming cherry blossoms. She'd learned the night before as we walked back that I was a Joseon-*jok*.

Yongju's eyes followed her hand stirring from her swollen belly to her too-perfect equation of a face. Mine did, too, for very different reasons.

Bakjun came out from our pit on his hands and knees. "How's our *nuna* doing?" He circled her like a hungry dog.

"Very well." She looked at Yongju. "*Dongmu,* thanks to you, I slept perfectly well. It was such a terrible night in the rain—I didn't know where to go."

Yongju flushed again. "You must be hungry, *dongmu.*"

She looked swiftly from the trees as gnarled as gnomes to our ragtag assembly emerging from the dugout. In that one sweeping glance that I would associate with her, she assessed how best to proceed.

Then she said quietly, "My baby is hungry," which seemed impossible. When she had come back to the cave with us the night before, all she had done was eat. Over our breakfast of stale bread and tiny potatoes that I had cajoled alive, I watched my friends go from trying to please her and making her comfortable to flirting wildly with her. I was confounded. It made no difference that she was years older than them or pregnant. Their comments got bolder, and Jangmi didn't discourage them. It was as if she wanted to keep her options open.

That was, until Cheolmin tucked his eggplant-shaped face over her shoulder and said, "Where's the father? When did he stick it to you?"

Her hands flew to her stomach as if to protect her baby.

"You little street beast!" Yongju cuffed Cheolmin across the head. "Don't ever talk to a woman like that again."

A sound rattled in Cheolmin's throat and his eyes narrowed. I tried to do my duty and distract him, pointing up to a bird's half-completed nest cradled in a pine tree. "There'll be other babies soon."

Everyone turned their full attention to the sparrow building a home, as if the nest was permanent.

I tried not to think about home or the past. And despite my stretches of guilt and gloom after I'd called my dad from the nearest village's public phone, reminding me of my messy life in America, the all-consuming task of securing the basic essentials was a topography so different from what I'd known that the past usually felt like a distant dream. I was also busy keeping up my part of an imagined bargain so that my friends wouldn't be tempted to get rid of me. I made myself chef, head gardener, wood collector. I started taking long solo trips to my former base and, as a last desperate measure, began asking for Missionary Kwon at the café he'd mentioned. I led my friends to edible roots and berries, treated burns, scouted for danger, and became their unofficial Mandarin teacher. There were dozens of species of plants to be flummoxed by, a bounty of bird-watching opportunities, my mouth to censor so I didn't give away the American part of me. I was surrounded by allies, puzzles of new knowledge, and my dulled, depressed senses were pricked alive by discomfort.

One day I splurged, dug into my emergency funds, and brought back dozens of cheap lamb skewers from the market stalls in town. We were careful with fires, and it was late at night when we headed farther out from our dugout so that no one would discover us. I started a tiny fire, more embers than a fire.

Yongju sat on a layer of newspapers beside Jangmi as if he were her guardian. He said, mainly in her direction, "On nights like this, it feels as if we're the only people remaining on the planet."

"No, *dongmu*," she said. The way she gazed at him made me nervous. "It's more as if the entire world is elsewhere and we've been forced out. I'm not just a lump of flesh waiting to get arrested. I'll walk to South Korea if I have to."

Yongju's eyes lingered on hers for a little too long. "I've considered it myself. But we don't have national identity cards if the police catch us on the way, and then there's the terrain we've never seen and the language, and so much more. It's impossible."

"Others have done it."

My mind raced for ways to wedge myself into their conversation. "You could marry for protection."

The guys had often talked about how their women could at least gain a modicum of safety in China by marrying, and envied them for this.

As soon as I spoke, Yongju cuffed my head for the first time. "You can't call that a marriage—the reality's more often a kidnapping and selling."

Before I could redeem myself, Jangmi made space on the flat-faced boulder that the others had taken to reserving for her and urged Bakjun to come closer to the fire. The next minute she said breathlessly, "You're wonderful!" when I fanned the fire from a sputter to a proper flame. I couldn't tell whether she was being sincere or calculating; it was hard to tell with her, and I wondered, even as she ruffled Namil's hair, then mine, what she was after. She was too sweet, too friendly; she reminded me of the girls at school who ignored me until they wanted tutoring before exams. But apparently everyone else was bedazzled by her.

In a word, I was jealous. She was naturally the center of attention, and it drove the rest of us out to the headlands of one another's sight, watering down our tight intimacy. At some moment that eluded me, Yongju and Jangmi had slipped from formal speech to speaking in *banmal,* though she was at least four years older than him and they hardly knew each other. And there was the way he looked intently at her, as if no one else was there but the two of them. He'd said that Jangmi reminded him of his mother. He'd said that he admired strong women. The way he made any excuse to be near her reminded me of me.

"You look like you need a drink." Namil, who was drunk as often as possible, offered me the bottle of strong Chinese liquor that was being passed around. The boys shared every scrap they had with one another; their generosity continually surprised me.

"You know I don't drink." I was underage and liked to draw thick black lines between right and wrong. I had great faith in the stability of those lines.

"I know, that's why I'm telling you to drink. If you did, you wouldn't be so . . . so—"

"The precise word is *uptight*," I said. "It's often been used to describe me."

"That's it! That's the word!" Namil twitched with laughter. I'd come to see that his happiness was more like a constant buzz of fear, and he was even happier when he was drunk.

"I shot down a crow once, with a rock." Gwangsu's pupils became so large and black that there was almost no white in his eyes. "This arm here's my lucky arm. Then I cooked up the bird and ate it. Really!"

"*Meojori!* You'd better pick juicier stories to tell than that. There's nothing to eat on a crow," said Bakjun.

"How would you know?"

Cheolmin said, "I know. I killed one when I was a kid just for fun and I pulled it all apart. I tell you, nothing but feathers."

I passed around a plastic bag of sunflower seeds given to me by a market vendor I'd run favors for. The boys had hands and maybe even hearts that made beef jerky look soft, but they were easily impressed when I made several throws in the dark and each time caught a seed in my mouth. Namil pulled out two packs of cigarettes that he'd bought with money he'd begged from a South Korean tourist, a feat he regularly managed. A South Korean could have provided more important things, like help and information, but the boys passed the packs back and forth as if nicotine was all that mattered, blowing smoke rings at one another and sighing with each inhale. I was always halfway with them and halfway elsewhere, Danny and Daehan the orphan at once.

"Is it enough for you?" said Yongju. "A cigarette from a South Korean tourist?"

Namil grinned and blew a perfect smoke ring. "*Dongmu,* it's a full pack, and foreign, too! Back home, I'd pick stubs off the ground and smoke them."

Yongju blew the smoke away. "Don't you want more? You can't live like this forever. You'll get older, and if the police catch you, as they inevitably will, you won't get a kid's treatment when you get sent back."

Namil pulled up his canvas pants and scratched at his legs, the skin cracked into dry cobweb patterns.

"That's the future," he said calmly, though he'd tensed at the word *police*. "I can't read the future."

Jangmi said, "The future's the only thing that matters."

I felt sick and surprised and guilty when, for a fleeting moment, I wished we had never met her. I nodded vigorously her way. "There must be all sorts of routes out, if you meet the right people."

Cheolmin's spit landed near my shoe. "You think you're so smart, so why don't you tell us how we can find them?"

Watch this, Namil mouthed at me, then scrambled behind the trees. It was as if getting to a safe country was so impossible for them that he didn't bother to give it another thought.

Namil reappeared a few minutes later behind Bakjun and said in a deep voice in Mandarin, "Security!"

Bakjun leaped up and hung briefly in midair like a basketball player. Bakjun, who had grown up sleeping near electricity conductors in the winters and breaking into storage sheds for food, had been caught in China twice, sent back, and escaped again—his body was a web of scars from all the beatings. When he saw it was Namil, he grabbed the bottle from Gwangsu, who was balancing it on his thigh with two hands, one of which looked as if a dog had bitten through it. Bakjun held the bottle as if to smash Namil in the head, a sudden surge of the violence and anger that lurked inside them. Only the others pulling him away stopped him.

I was listening for something else.

That was when I heard it for sure, a noise outside of our circle. I stood up and listened to the forest. When pine needles crackled, I held up my hand.

"There's someone out there!" I pointed at the trees across from me. "Who's there?"

The others scattered before I finished my sentence, fleeing kidnappers, security, whoever might be after them. The underbrush thrashed, then two people stepped out into the light of the fire, an elderly couple who could have been our grandparents. Their faces were bruised purple and their hands so filthy that they looked half mole, half human. When the *halmeoni* let go of the lapels of her coat I saw a wide tear across the front of her blouse. Apart from the homeless drug addicts in downtown Los Angeles, I had never seen elderly people in such a sorry state. Their shuffle forward was more an exhausted cringe, as if they expected anyone, even me, a mere kid, to unleash vitriol their way. Their animal smell grew stronger as they approached me and I soon saw why. The man was bleeding from the mouth, and when he opened it to speak, a thick sap trickled out. There were great gaps where his teeth should have been and one incisor hung from his gums by a fleshy string.

I didn't know what else to do except to hand the woman a soiled towel and promise her some lamb skewers.

"My husband can't eat them. He can't eat anything anymore."

I was shocked, wondering whether her husband would bleed to death, and raced through my limited medical knowledge to see if there was anything I could do. From the shadows where they were watching, the others slowly returned.

Yongju took her hands in his. "Halmeoni, what happened?" His voice was velvet, as if she were actually his grandmother.

"We've been walking for hours." The *halmeoni* clutched his hands. "The farmer we were working for was—he was being inappropriate with me. My husband tried to stop him, but the *ganna saekki* used a hammer on his teeth, and now the bleeding won't stop."

She cried silently as if the sound itself had been beaten out of her.

Yongju gave them a tin of stream water he had collected that afternoon and had them sit close to the fire. But as the others began to yawn, the couple hovered, waiting, until the *halmeoni* finally said, "If you have a shelter, and we could stay, just for the night . . ."

Yongju lowered his head. "We have no room. I'm sorry."

I recoiled with shame. The *harabeoji* bled and the *halmeoni* cried, but wanting to agree with the others, I stayed quiet. And I called myself a Christian. I was beginning to ask myself what that really meant.

Before we crawled back into our dugout, we roughed up the bed of pine needles and leaves behind us and erased our tracks, then pulled the camouflaged screen over. When I closed my eyes that night, I saw the man's bleeding mouth, the frightened pits of his eyes. In the morning my wish had come true. Jangmi was gone. She had taken every lightweight, useful item in our shelter with her.

Part III

Safe

12

Yongju

These were my first images of the safe house: The gas lantern that Missionary Kwon had me raise above our heads that turned us into skulls without bodies, as he introduced us to our caretaker Missionary Lee. Missionary Lee's ink-smudged fingers sweeping across his face and the blue streak they left on his nose. The voices of trees caressing the two-story brick building. The boys' faces glowing with hope.

Missionary Kwon had driven us past a town that thinned into a desolate fringe of construction projects, a rusted crane, then whittled down into barren country roads. One road led to a bridge built across a trickle of a stream to a gate, behind which was our building. Though I was a storm of feeling, the night was as calm and cool as a sheet of glass. The yard of weeds as thick as a vagabond's stubble. Then we were shuttled up exposed cement blocks that served as stairs into a common room, down a narrow corridor, and into the few unfinished rooms that we would live in.

Daehan said, "Wait for me!" though there was nowhere to go, and scrambled to my side. As if I could protect him. As if I could protect anyone.

Missionary Kwon extended his arms, his smile as heavy as a large stone. He told us that this God of theirs loved us. "You see?" he said. "God always provides."

In the lantern's light, he gave us a lengthy introduction to Missionary Lee.

"I'm so happy to see you all here safe!" Missionary Lee's voice was so frail that it seemed to sink into his elephantine girth. "I've been praying for you every day since Missionary Kwon told me about you.

"You must be Yongju, and you Daehan, and you Bakjun." As he called out our names one by one, he embraced each of us though our clothes were crusty and we stank of alcohol.

"I'll have to document this." Missionary Kwon directed us to stand against a slab of scarred concrete and pulled out a camera from his bag.

I felt as if I were in a war movie, a prisoner with infested hair about to be executed by American soldiers. Which reminded me of my *eomeoni*. Everything reminded me of my *eomeoni*.

"You think I like this?" Missionary Kwon said, though no one had said anything. "Sponsors want evidence. There's not a thing we can do about it." He took several photographs and encouraged us to look solemn through the camera's clicking.

Late that night after we had our first baths, he took another set of photos of us cleaned up and told us to smile. The camera—the first time I'd seen such a camera—spat out squares of glossy white paper that turned into our ghostly images within minutes. The boys crowded around to see themselves, the same way they had after Missionary Kwon had taken photos of us in the mountains. Namil was grinning in nearly every shot, but his eyes stayed mournful, and Cheolmin's skin was flaky and reptilian, but my image alarmed me most. My gaze was gaunt, ashen; loss had passed over my face and I had become a different person.

In the safe house the clock showed me what time it was, the calendar I marked off each day told me the date. I saw time passing as spindly leaves formed on the oak trees surrounding the building. The sun and the moon swept into the room where the dozen *yo* we slept on were folded and stacked in the corner, still bearing the imprint of our bodies. I tried to think of the sun as a promise, a daily present that broke through the trees. I dreaded the rising moon, a time when all the people I had lost returned to me.

In the safe house there was always Missionary Lee and occasionally Missionary Kwon. Kwon was the actual God that filled our days. He had our rotten teeth pulled and ragged fingernails cleaned up, the loamy smell thick on our skin scrubbed away, until he disappeared to manage another dozen shelters. I knew power, had grown up around its black suits and unhurried air and tinted car windows. This somber man never strained to get our attention; we moved according to his wishes. I began hearing the measured rhythm of his voice in my dreams.

There was so much to do in the safe house, and so much that had been invented for us to do. There was the hall to sweep every morning after sunrise prayer. We took care not to snag our house slippers on the unfinished cement floor and gazed out the door's eyehole, fearing a stranger's eye would meet ours though no one was ever there. We tried that door a dozen times a day though we knew it was locked from the outside—to protect us, they said—and collected trash since most of it could be reused. We recycled leftovers from breakfast for lunch and what was left from lunch for dinner.

We, we, we—that was what I had become.

Still I felt attached to this little nothing—the square of light, the faint comfort of meat bone soup, the freedom from the dank cave—this remote promise that someday my life would matter again, just a little, to me.

We were finally safe.

13

Danny

I woke up before the sun was out, surrounded by boys' bodies twisted together like pretzels. Most important, Yongju's back was inches from me. Like every morning during our month in the safe house, his warm, nutty smell enveloped me before I opened my eyes.

Sure, you could have built another Mount Sinai with the total sum of our discomforts. But I'd gotten used to the bucket for a bathroom, the lack of electricity, Missionary Lee's two-tiered snores that drilled straight through the wall, and the random scream and gnashing of teeth from the boys. But I was still surprised when I woke up to Missionary Kwon's broad chin and the waft of his pine needle soap. His weekly appearances at the safe house fell on random days, and when his looming shadow shook me by the shoulder, I wasn't prepared and I slapped away his hand.

It clamped down on mine. He said, "Wake up, there're supplies, and I've set up the bath."

I crawled upright, wanting yet dreading the bimonthly bath ritual, myself knuckled into the first floor's pink tub pulled out from beneath cardboard boxes. There I would be, folded into what had probably held a frothing vat of kimchi.

When he moved away to wake up Yongju, the room became musky again with the scent of boys. It brought me to my senses, and I immediately bowed my head until the other boys were awake. I'd practically grown up in the church and I was determined to stay inside the maps I understood, reliable black-and-white ones of Christian and heathen, the right route and the wrong. My maps didn't include school or family anymore.

I followed the others down the concrete steps slick from last night's rain. The air choked with pollutants was still a welcome contrast to our room, which smelled like you had your nose up an armpit. None of it bothered me much. I was awed by their uncomplicated, generous acceptance of me. Shut up in that hermetically sealed building, I expected nothing less than to be reformed by the missionaries.

But all I saw were the constellations of goose bumps across Yongju's exposed neck.

The half-moon highlighted the fine hairs standing up on his neck and the triangle of his back hunched through the padded coat. He had been feverish since the night before, his upper lip beaded with sweat, and I had to resist reaching out and touching that vulnerable arch of his back.

"Careful." He tilted his head my way, though I was taking every precaution and gripping the cold stair rail with both hands.

"Stay still, *hyeong*." I wrapped my striped scarf around his neck as he had once done for me, then tugged my ski hat over his head. Only this much. I was still innocent. "We lose nearly ten percent of our heat from our head."

From behind me, Cheolmin muttered, "Ten percent, my ass."

It was no secret that only Cheolmin had his reservations about me. You had to push back with people like that, I'd learned, so I said, "We can test it out on you, if you like."

Missionary Kwon said in a warning voice, "Boys, keep your voices down." He opened the trunk of the car parked in the yard.

He could have bellowed out if he wanted to; no one was around to hear us for at least a mile. There was a charisma about his quiet confidence, which was the way I imagined Jesus addressing his fishers of men, and I found my voice dropping to the decibel of moving grass. He awed me, from his old-fashioned three-piece suit to his hair parted in the middle that made him look like an itinerant nineteenth-century Methodist pastor.

We knew the weekly routine by now. Without further instruction we carried the boxes of food and sacks of ice up to our supply room and half the plastic containers of water to the first floor. The others moved slowly, gazing at the moon, the clouds and trees, the outlines of hills, as if they'd forgotten what the world looked like. Yongju and I, who Missionary Kwon had decided were the most detail-oriented of the group, carried the burners and the largest steel pots downstairs to the first floor. We heated up our precious water supply for the bath, using equally precious gas canisters.

I insisted, as I had the time before, on being the last to wash. I knew they appreciated it. Naturally the water wasn't changed, so by the time my turn came the bath was a muddy soup that was at best lukewarm. I, a self-declared clean freak, skimmed off the film of dead skin and dirt floating on the surface, then immersed myself in the swampy water, curled up knees to nipples. I found myself thinking of my mom and how she scrubbed my back when I was a kid, still only a mom to me then and not a woman. My stomach cramped up as I thought about my parents, though I'd called my dad to tell him about my general plans before following Missionary Kwon. I should have returned home, but I didn't. I couldn't. I didn't want to.

How could I when Yongju squatted beside the tub and began wordlessly scrubbing my back with a sandpapery *ttaeh sugeon,* stripping off layers of dead skin?

That morning when we sat for sunrise prayer with Missionary Lee, I was at my customary spot on the floor beside Yongju. We had become an inseparable pair at the two lacquered *saang* that were our only tables, like Batman and Robin. The Monkey King and Monk Xuanzang. I played the sidekick perfectly, and no one suspected anything. I tried my mightiest to focus on the posters of Noah's paired-up zebras and giraffes, Jesus feeding bread and fish to hundreds. Even the plastic *dotjari* that covered up our cement floors, usually used on picnics, was printed with an image of David and Goliath. I should have been at ease, surrounded by familiar stories and knowing I was the only one who would truly be safe if the police discovered us. Even Missionary Lee, who risked a long prison sentence if he was caught harboring North Koreans, grabbed the arm nearest him and dug in with his fingernails whenever Missionary Kwon opened the front door. But all I felt was turbulence.

Immediately after prayer, Missionary Lee set his hands on the shelf of his belly, his eyes open so wide that the cholesterol deposits in his sclera bugged out. "Why didn't Missionary Kwon wake me up? Why didn't any of you tell me he was here? There are important things we have to discuss."

His multiple chins tucked into his chest. The shaggy-haired sheepdog of a man who looked as old as Abraham was appallingly bad at hiding his hurt feelings. There was also something ancient and severely good about this retired schoolteacher from South Korea, the kind of man I imagined God would entrust with a tablet of commandments. He could have lived comfortably on his pension, cycling and fishing with his family and doing whatever else retired people do, but his faith had brought him to this hazardous work. I longed for a simple, if arduous, map of life like the one he followed.

"Apparently Missionary Kwon didn't want to disturb your sleep." I found myself checking for Yongju's reaction. I added, "He knows how hard you've been working."

Cheolmin drummed his chest with his fingers and snorted, but Yongju nodded, approving of behavior that might improve our standing. Missionary Kwon had promised to send them to true safety in a third country within a few months, as soon as funding became available.

The missionary flushed and thumped the *saang*'s enameled

cranes. "God is watching us, so you should keep your backs straight"—meaning a respectful ramrod—"your legs crossed and tucked"—under our numb thighs—"and your hands flat on the *saang* as we start our lesson." He was full of empty threats.

We weren't twenty minutes into the lesson when Cheolmin slumped onto the table and erupted into snores. I wasn't surprised when the missionary said gently, "Let him sleep." He patted Cheolmin's buzzed hair, recently doused with lice-killing chemicals like all of ours. "He probably didn't get any rest last night."

"I don't understand." Namil flicked away a balled-up gray mass he had picked out of his navel. "Where's this God? Where's he live now?"

"Live?" Missionary Lee blinked rapidly, his window dressing of eyelashes almost white in the light.

I felt a little sorry for him.

He continued with the lesson without answering. His voice was as dry as a communion wafer, and his teaching style could turn Daniel and the lion into a run-in with a kitten; it wasn't the most impressive of sailings. But I admired his unwavering sincerity.

Me, I was wavering. I made monkey faces whenever Yongju caught me looking at him, slipped on the *dotjari* and fell at his feet so that he would pull me up, and made shadow puppets with my hand in front of the candlelight before bed. I turned myself into a fool. Anything at all to stay close to him.

Other times, I dangled facts and names off a fishing pole and waited for him to take the bait. My one reliable strength was the computer chip of my head. He would ask me throughout the day,

"What's the Pentecost?" or "Who is this Steven Pinker?" and most recently, "What's string theory? You don't need to tell me where you learned these things—you don't need to tell me anything about yourself you don't want me to know, but I need to know the world we weren't allowed to know . . . just in case." He swallowed, the diamond of his Adam's apple dancing.

At lunch the next day, I raced between the kitchen and the common room and, being twice as fast as the others, ended up doing over a quarter of the prep duties. "You're a rocket!" Yongju said, which made me sprint even faster.

The two *saang* were heavy with vegetable dishes that we had seasoned the day before, a pot of steaming white rice, an equally large pot of *dwenjang* stew with soybeans and tofu bobbing at the top, and spicy pork that had been kept on ice. The boys couldn't take their eyes off the fatty curls of pork. Their swallows made hard punctuation marks during the grace.

"Amen!" said Namil, and shoved a tower of rice into his mouth by the spoonful, then another.

"Namil, I've been meaning to tell you," I said. "I thought you might like to know, in all probability, you're wearing a woman's sweater." He was also wearing bobby socks, but I let that one go.

He grinned, showing the clumps of rice stuck in the gaps of his teeth. "Really?" He rubbed at his chest with two hands. "So that's why it felt so good."

The others hooted. Missionary Lee gasped and Yongju, blushing, said, "This isn't the streets," with the sharpest look he could manage, which sent Namil diving back into the cheap ceramic bowl.

The sound of scraping chopsticks and spoons could have blocked out a marching band, but I still heard what was on their minds: When would the missionaries send them to South Korea?

Missionary Lee poured water into his bowl at the end of the meal, as if he were a Buddhist monk doing *gongyang bari*. After he drank the remains, he held the bowl close to his face with both hands and licked it clean, his sad bloodhound's eyes saying, How can I waste when so many go hungry?

Yongju kept his gaze on Missionary Lee as he scraped the last grain of rice out of his bowl. "It must be nearly time for us to leave," he said, as if it were an afterthought.

Missionary Lee flushed. "Missionary Kwon will know." It was his go-to answer for all of Yongju's many questions. Then he heaved himself toward the storage room, the room rumbling under his weight.

I wondered if the missionary knew more than he was letting on.

The others stretched, barely awake after their heroic struggle to stay seated all morning. The only motive for their good behavior was food. Namil's and Bakjun's palms were already cupped and waiting for the South Korean Choco Pies that Missionary Lee occasionally gave them if they behaved. The cheap fifty-cents-a-pop snack made me long for industrial-strength toothpaste, but as soon as the missionary came back and handed them out, even Yongju unwrapped the bright red packaging as if the chocolate-covered marshmallow cream pie was an archaeological find.

Bakjun held his up like a squirrel guarding an acorn in winter. "I remember the first time I had one of these after crossing. Never had anything so good."

If junk food was the height of their pleasure, I wondered if it was truly possible to imagine their world across the river. I tried to participate. "I heard that Choco Pies are hot on the Pyongyang black market—the *jangmadang*," I corrected myself, and used their word for it. "Companies give them out to people from your country working in Kaesong for South Korean companies, then the sweets leak out and get resold. Some higher-ups are making a lot of cash."

"I don't understand a word you're saying." Namil cheerfully licked his fingers one by one. "It's all Han characters to me."

"Of course your government wouldn't tell you about Kaesong." I explained that a small group of their people worked for South Korean companies but were not allowed to leave the special district within Kaesong again. "All governments, ultimately, are in collusion with one another."

"Collusion? What's collusion?" said Namil.

"We would never work for those American lackeys!" Cheolmin the Troublemaker—my private moniker for him—said angrily in front of South Korean passport holder Missionary Lee, though his front teeth were streaked with the Choco Pie made in that very country.

Bakjun, who had slowly gone from listless to angry with his supply of cigarettes and alcohol cut off, smacked the table. "I don't care if they give good handouts and make good snacks. I'd cut my balls off than work for an American lackey."

The missionary's hands flapped to his mouth. "If you don't stop, I'll have to discipline you! Remember, whatever you say is always in the presence of the Lord."

"Maybe I got it wrong," I said.

I focused on the gooey marshmallow. I tried to understand what it must be like for my friends to be inundated with so much new data. I suddenly missed my mom, and myself, the person I was with her, even with my parents' messy, soiled marriage. Then Yongju smiled and roughed up my hair, and everything else fell away, and I only felt shame and longing.

A few days later we had our first visitors, a couple wearing the brightest shades of spring between them. Their church meant something to me. When I was fourteen, Salvation Church had sponsored a trip for disadvantaged youth to South Korea—that was my family!—and brought me to Seoul, a city that was dotted with neon red crosses. My breath had stopped when I saw the church's vaulted ceiling, which seemed to rise higher than a canopy of redwood trees straight into the arms of God. But these representatives supporting the safe house were the last people I wanted to lay eyes on; the Christian leadership diaspora was tiny, and with my luck, they might know my mom.

We'd been scrubbed and polished before noon, our hair trimmed and nails cut. Our jerseys, shorts, and rolled-up jeans had been swapped for checkerboard button-down shirts and tan slacks. The other guys had their radar on the cake box cradled in Mrs. Bang's arms, but you could have cut through Yongju's tension with a knife. I hung back behind Missionary Lee, who was hovering in the rear. I wished I knew what he thought of this exhibit A we'd been turned into.

Missionary Kwon handed his jacket to Yongju after taking out the three cell phones he routinely exchanged for others. "It's for your security," he'd first explained in his ever-grave voice, impressing me with the serious nature of his mission. I got that the missionary needed those phones to juggle his humanitarian, religious, and gang contacts, which were required for everything from fake I.D.s to crossing the border, but I didn't feel comfortable when he began directing us like a CEO with his employees in front of the couple.

"We feel so blessed to finally be here." Mrs. Bang's smile was as broad and plain as a garbanzo bean, and she wore her hair in a skullcap of curls. She set the curlicued lemon chiffon on the *saang*.

"I'd be thankful for a blessed kiss, one from each of you," she added, and tapped her cheek.

Naturally we cooperated after Missionary Kwon nudged Yongju. Her husband, who'd been introduced as a church elder, looked apologetic as we stepped forward one at a time.

"We're so excited to be here with you." He spoke without the self-importance that most elders wore like an emperor's robe. "We've been praying hard for this moment."

His wife piped up, "God's kingdom is for the poor and the powerless—I promise, he has special plans for you."

She turned to Missionary Kwon. "How do you keep so many shelters functioning? It's really fantastic, just incredible work. The Lord is truly working through you."

"The Lord is working through all of us, all the time."

His eyes took on a faraway look, as if he was in the presence of the Lord alone. I admired the grace that seemed to emerge from his faith; I had begun to question the nature of my own. He abruptly returned, frowning as he looked from us to Mr. and Mrs. Bang.

"Your honorable church made this venture possible by lending us the building—really the only safe place to keep boys their age. We're merely janitors doing the necessary work. And this young man you see here keeps them in line." Missionary Kwon gave Yongju's shoulder a firm squeeze. "Otherwise these kinds of boys would be too dangerous to shelter."

He nodded to Yongju, who led them down the dark corridor. "This is where we sleep." He gestured to the neat stacks of *yo* and pillows in the corner and the plastic frame hanger heavy with our clothes. They continued down the hall past the room where Missionary Lee slept, then to the storage room stocked with rice, corn, and canned goods. Yongju retreated there whenever he needed privacy.

After prayers, Mrs. Bang hoisted slices of cake onto paper plates and passed them down like an assembly line. Gwangsu's tongue washed over his teeth like windshield wipers and Cheolmin rubbed his frostbitten foot, the way he always did when anticipating something. The cake slices were gone in three swallows. Only Yongju didn't disappoint me; he nibbled his one bite at a time, savoring it.

"*Trauma*'s the only word for it." Missionary Kwon set a hand on his heart, as if it was hurting. "Entire villages of women are bought and sold. There's even a house church pastor who turned in the North Korean refugees in his congregation and collected the Chinese government's cash reward."

The cake was the other boys' universe; only Yongju and I were really listening. The missionary gave a summary of each of our lives, with details that emphasized how pitiful it was to be North Korean. He even introduced me as a homeless *kkotjaebi* from Musan whose parents had been part of the underground church, though I'd told him that I was a Joseon-*jok* orphan. Namil spat out a chunk of cake at the flagrant lie. I was ashamed; I'd been made even more of an imposter than I already was.

"Outside of this one"—Missionary Kwon nodded my way—"none of them had known of the Lord's word before they met me."

"You've devoted your life to these poor North Koreans." Mrs. Bang's thin nose quivered. "They owe you their lives. I heard how you used to lead refugees out of China across the Gobi Desert. You could have died."

He said solemnly, "And the jungles of Southeast Asia, but I'm on their radar now. Too many of us have been caught; I can't put any more lives at risk. The trouble is, trustworthy smugglers are as rare as the Hope diamond."

Missionary Lee's head bobbed up and down, his slice of cake long gone. He said shyly, "There's been too many lives at risk already." It was the first complete sentence he'd ventured in front of the Bangs.

"You're thinking of Missionary Lim," said Missionary Kwon. "I saw him the last time I was back."

They continued to talk, and I got that this Missionary Lim had sold the only residence he owned in Seoul and spent that money to personally escort North Koreans to a safe third country.

Mrs. Bang said, "Is it true what I heard—that after they caught him, the Chinese tortured him until his heart stopped and he was declared dead?"

Missionary Kwon nodded. "He weighed forty-five kilos when he finally made it to Seoul. An eighty-kilo man, originally as large as Missionary Lee. He said when he came back to life, they started torturing him again."

"It's been two years now since our diplomats got him out, but he'll never be the same man."

"It's not just him, either," said Missionary Lee. "His wife and children, think of their suffering."

"China." Mr. Bang's narrow shoulders jumped at each word. "No country's brave enough to challenge it."

"But why?" Yongju interjected, looking baffled. "Why do people risk their lives this way?"

The smooth mask of Missionary Kwon's face softened. "Because we believe in God."

The thought of so many risking their lives for other people moved me. I wanted to be like them, to have my DNA restructured and become someone capable of such faith. To conquer my own desires and live for something greater than the self. But my awe diminished when Missionary Kwon showed them the photos he'd taken in the cave, with our scabby faces and our dirt-caked clothes, then photos of a man and a woman sitting cross-legged with tiny Bibles spread open in their laps, talking to an elderly couple. Then came photos of a squinting man at a guard post and others in front of North Korean statues, obviously across the river.

Missionary Kwon said, "I told you about them earlier, the ones we taught who returned to do the Lord's work in North Korea. One of my contacts went in posing as a Chinese tourist—which is dangerous!—to confirm it."

While Mr. Bang talked about bringing the Lord's light to that dark world, I tried to stop the pounding in my head. I was so confused. I couldn't stop staring at the photos of the couple, apparently part of the underground church in North Korea. Was that Missionary Kwon's plan for my friends, too?

"The Lord guided them—it was their choice to return. I'd never force that on anyone." Missionary Kwon took the closest hand—Yongju's—in his. "The Bible's your friend. And you'll know the entire book like a friend once you've completed your studies with us."

Yongju pulled his hand away. "What does that mean?"

"It's standard practice." Irritation crossed Missionary Kwon's face, then disappeared. "How could you leave without knowing the Lord's word?"

My pencil splintered in my hand. "You mean you're holding them hostage until they memorize the whole book?"

Namil snapped, "The whole book?"

Cheolmin's half-closed eyes popped open. "What do you mean, the whole book?"

Missionary Kwon gave me a look of warning. "You'll be blessed. A year, three years, however long it takes, the Lord's word can only change your life for the better."

Cheolmin flipped through all six hundred and twenty-eight pages of the Bible, then shoved it away from him. The Bangs smiled, but they avoided meeting our eyes.

Yongju rubbed at the Roman numeral on the last page. "Most of them can barely read.

"You promised we'd be here a month, a few months at most, while you raised the funds, Missionary Kwon." His voice shook as he clasped Missionary Kwon's hands. "Please. I promise to go to church and read the Bible in Seoul, anywhere you send me."

"You'll be surrounded by the devil's many temptations, but here where you need the Lord the most, he will find you. I've witnessed the miraculous change in so many of you."

"But my family. How will I find my family—"

Yongju's beautiful head bowed to the *saang* as he shook with silent sobs. All his hopes hinged on making his way to South Korea, a country that equaled information and resources. I felt his helplessness and the way his family must have seemed to be drifting further away from him. I wanted to do something, anything, to stop those tears.

Missionary Lee looked to the left and right at us. "Missionary Kwon?" His voice was a whisper.

Silence finally became impossible. I said, "We might not know God's will, but he just might not have brought them all this precious way only to leave them rotting in China!"

Missionary Lee pinched my foot under the *saang,* but I didn't want to stop; I didn't want to ever stay silent again.

"What's more, if that couple you sent back get caught and are executed," I said, slamming the table for effect, "you will become a murderer."

Missionary Lee gasped. Missionary Kwon reached across the table, grabbed my hands, and stopped their thumping. He said, "That's enough!"

The Bangs were too shocked to notice that I'd slipped up and said "them" and not "us." But something else—maybe recognition that what I said was true? or shame?—flashed like a bat's shadow across Mrs. Bang's face.

Missionary Kwon's words came at a furious clip. We had only been with him for a few weeks and were transitioning. Missionary Lee was new and though knowledgeable, he had a soft heart and was too indulgent. As Missionary Kwon regained his composure, he ruffled my hair, saying, "*Jaashik,* you'll come around." But I didn't believe in him anymore.

He added, "You little rascals. Someday you'll understand that though the body may be safe in South Korea, we're keeping you here to save your soul."

Yongju shuddered. That small hunched movement moved me. I wasn't the only one. Missionary Lee rose and gave him a clumsy hug. He said, "I'm so sorry, my son."

Mrs. Bang folded her arms tightly across her chest.

"You should know that with all the border crackdowns, it's much harder for your people to cross than before." She looked at us with reproach, as if a stranglehold border should have made them grateful to be locked up indefinitely. "Look, here you are, safe! God is more powerful than any government."

Later I learned of other organizations, including some Christian groups, who moved people quickly out of China. Many anonymous good folks undertook the dangerous work while governments talked about North Korean human rights but were too trade-happy with China to act. But my friends were Missionary Kwon's charges. For them it would be Genesis, Exodus, Leviticus, and so on, until they were converted. Unless I did something about it.

14

Jangmi

A week after I left the mountains I was betrayed by a Joseon-jok woman who promised to help me, then sold me to a local gang. In the crowded city that seemed large enough to hide in, the woman had given me a job with actual pay at her eatery. I was so grateful, but within a few days of working in the kitchen, men in a van seized me and forced me into a basement den.

When they stepped back, the first person I saw in the mildewed basement was a young girl with heavy bangs. She ran straight into the knot of my belly, this girl about Byeol's height. She reminded me of Seongsik and the life we had cobbled together. I held her to me as one of the men behind me coughed.

"Go back inside, Suhyeon!" said a woman with brassy dyed-red hair coiled up into a bird's nest.

Her voice crackled with displeasure, and she yanked the girl into a private room near the entrance. I never saw the girl again.

The *ajumma* the men had said would take care of me was a stern terror with a black fuzz above her upper lip. Her gauzy skirt and a billowing jacket that increased her generous size made her appear even more formidable.

"What am I supposed to do with her?" She prodded my stomach.

"Trust me, there's a niche market for women like her," said one of the men with a colorful serpent tattoo winding up his neck. He looked like one of the gang members that had terrified us at home.

"What about later? What will happen *later*? I don't want trouble."

"Shut up with the questions and do what you're told," he said. "That's what you're paid for."

"All right, all right," she muttered, dropping her gaze.

I wanted to scream; I wanted to claw away the walls as if they were paper. I wanted to reverse three generations of decisions so that my grandparents would die fighting against American imperialists and Nam Joseon lackeys, and give our family a hero's *seongbun,* so we could live differently. But looking back wasn't going to help my baby, so I calmed myself as some of the men left and others headed down the hall. I looked for any routes for future escape, but there was only the one locked door leading out.

"We'll want more vitamins in your diet." The *ajumma* inspected me. "I don't want any sicknesses."

A pitiful sound escaped me. I couldn't believe it was from me.

"Dear, it could be worse." She patted my arm. "Plenty of your people service twenty men a day, real men. You're only servicing them online."

She unlocked one of the cubicle rooms. A baby-faced girl with a turned-up nose, introduced as Miyeon, emerged in a robe of scarlet and vermilion, her legs bare. She crossed her arms over her thin chest.

"*Eoh-meonah,* Eonni!" This girl, who didn't look eighteen, caressed my stomach. "What will you do? What will you ever do?"

"The same thing you do, for some very special customers," the *ajumma* said. "She's by the bathroom. You know the routine."

After the *ajumma* left me in Miyeon's care, we sat on the bed, the only place to sit.

"I'm from Yanggang province," she offered in a rapid, high-pitched voice.

"I'm from North Hamgyong province."

"Me, I thought I would cross, earn good money for my family working at a Joseon-*jok* restaurant. That's what the broker told me. But they brought me here."

"I was sold into marriage." I was too ashamed to say that when I first crossed I'd agreed to being sold.

She confirmed that the dozen locked doors lining the hallway outside held more of our women, we who had grown up with our skirts hemmed below our knees and sleeves covering our shoulders. Most had been sold to Chinese men our grandfathers' age, tricked by brokers, or kidnapped. She pressed her bony knees to her chest when I asked, and confirmed that there was no way to escape. The best way to stay out of trouble here, she said, was to be invisible.

While she babbled, I took stock of her bed, the clock and the mirror, the computer stand, the computer. That was all there was in the tiny room.

"But why am I here? What do we have to do?" I asked.

She took my hands in hers. "You'll . . . you'll have to take your clothes off for men on camera. It's all done by computer. You been long in China?"

I shook my head. Tried to keep my breathing regular. If I opened my mouth a scream would come out.

"Do you know what a computer is?"

I nodded. "The man I was first sold to had one."

"There are some real perverts out there, Eonni. I'm sorry." She bit down on her lower lip, leaving a track of peony-tinted lipstick across her uneven front teeth. "It seems impossible, but you will get used to it."

Her words became disordered fragments as the number grew in my head of the days, months, even years the women had been enslaved. I thought of the flower girls in our country, selling their bodies to men. But I was an overripe fruit; I couldn't believe that men descended to such measures.

Miyeon showed me to my room, with an identical frame bed and computer squeezed into it. This was where I would take the South Korean men's calls. Strip off my clothes and do what they wanted me to. I collapsed onto the bed, short shallow breaths escaping me.

"I can't do this," I managed.

She squeezed my hand and said again, "Oh, Eonni." She said

nothing more than that. "Older Sister." As if recognizing me was all she could promise.

I was locked in like the rest of them. At first I pummeled the door to my room until my knuckles were raw. The door, the color of green of bleached tea leaves, was covered in long scratches. Nail marks. My voice withered, for our doors opened only when the *ajumma* decided to open them. There was little to distract me except for the clock ticking opposite the wall and two heart-shaped pillows tied to the lumpy bed. With my ear pressed to the thin partitions, I listened for the low murmur of other girls. In the monitor I saw myself looking at me and wondered who else was looking.

We were given a pill with every meal, every day. The *ajumma* said, "I want your skin to glow with health!" No matter how many pills we took, nothing changed our sallow, underground look. A tin tray came to my door loaded with rice, vegetables, a watery *dwenjang guk*. There was room inspection and cleaning duties. A black-suited man at the main door changed off with other men at the twelfth hour. Other black suits banged in and out through the front door, stinking of cigarette smoke, and headed to the back room stuffed with couches where they played cards and, occasionally, called for a favorite girl. They were the only people the *ajumma* listened to.

Every day the computer screen lit up blue, then white, and a man glowed into focus. My first client was a man with gray hair and the face of a twenty-year-old. He didn't waste time. As soon as he appeared on the screen, he said, "Why's your robe on? I didn't pay for a robe. I can go to the department store for that."

All of them were from Nam Joseon. The Dear Leader was right about one thing: It was a nation of sick people. I kept my eyes fixed on the window to the man's right. I told myself that the sky was still there and real, waiting for me.

I thought I would go mad. I endured. The computer's camera followed me. I woke up to it and slept to it. Always, I felt someone watching me. I was caught inside the blank screen for all those eyes to touch. Nam Joseon men in navy suits, men in white undershirts beached in their chairs, naked men, hairy men, men with the high-pitched voices of women. Men who desired pregnant women.

Only my baby mattered. I stroked the tight drum of my stomach, the beautiful life of four months that knew nothing of this room. I pictured a curled fist of webbed fingers, a giant bean of a body, and carried love and fear inside me.

Within a few weeks I resorted to the only plan possible. I started with a man whittled down to a chopstick. My stomach had swelled and my breasts were heavier now and tender at their tips. The man shyly sneaked looks at me, this shell in which I was protecting two beating hearts, and said, "You could be a pregnant schoolgirl."

He was old enough to have a daughter in school. I missed Eomma. I kept one leg up, one arm curved across my waist.

"Is that what you like, pregnant schoolgirls?"

I slipped off the robe.

He nodded and rambled on nervously. "Women are too skinny these days. It's all that dieting. If you eat tomatoes all day, it's a tomato diet. Watermelons, a watermelon diet."

"What's a diet?"

He laughed and explained dieting to me. The concept was shocking. But Nam Joseon was also a country with more cars than bicycles, where people freely traveled without punishment. It wasn't real to me yet, but I knew it was a safe country where a future was possible. Though its people were sick, I wanted to go there.

"Help me," I said finally to him, as I would to each of my men, and waited for his response.

One of the girls slit her slender wrist with a shard of mirror. The *ajumma* took our mirrors away. One moved like a broken ox. One girl wrapped herself in a padded coat that hid her body of fish bones whenever the *ajumma* allowed us to pace the halls. My memory comes in fragments. Nothing is chronological. In my sleep I walked through the paint-peeled walls of our underground fortress, out into the white sunlight and back across the frozen river toward home. When the girl used the mirror on herself, I thought it could have been me. Maybe it was the end of my second month—or the third?—when the man I had waited for arrived.

I glimpsed a faint gold cross hanging on the wall behind him, took the risk, and told him where I was from. He viewed me calmly from his leather chair, as if he had already known before he called. The man I would later call Missionary Kwon fixed his gaze on me until I—even I!—had to look away.

Finally he said, "I'm a powerful man. I can do anything. I could buy your freedom for you."

I looked behind me, but of course there was only a wall.

"Why would you do that for me? You don't know me."

I didn't really believe this. A man would do many things for a stranger if she was young and beautiful enough.

"You're not the first group of girls I've found this way. I've raised enough money this time to get many of you out."

He settled back into the chair that rose with imperial gravity behind him. His frozen face looked incapable of expression.

I tried to hide my excitement. "What do you want from me?"

"What could you possibly give me that I would want?" He thought about it for a moment, then said, "Take off your clothes, in case there's trouble."

I jerked the cord loose and let the robe fall, surrounding me in a sea of scarlet. His gaze remained steady despite my ripe shape. He didn't seem particularly interested, at least not in the way I was used to. I felt desperate for his attention—to use my little power not to become a pregnant woman sent back across the river with a baby believed to be Chinese-born, of impure blood.

He said, "Why did you cross?"

His question cornered me. "Who are you, really?"

He wagged a finger at me. "I'm here to help you. Are you always so suspicious?"

I crossed my legs. "I have no reason to trust you."

His image wavered on the screen, then steadied again. "Do you have a choice?"

Of course I didn't.

"How long have they held you?"

"Someone could be listening."

"The server's routed through South Korea—what your people call Nam Joseon."

"How do you know?"

"It's my job to know these things. So? Your crossing? There are people who need to know these things before I can do anything for you."

It didn't matter which side of the river I was on. Men asked the questions and women answered. Maybe that is all power is: the right to demand and expect answers. But before I learned what he could do for me, I heard someone at the door and the man ended the video call.

Sometime after the third meal that divided our day, the man called again.

I spoke rapidly this time, mostly telling the truth. The person I exaggerated for him was pathetic and needy, though my real situation was desperate enough without my flourishes. Wasn't he allured, moved by pity? Convinced I was worth saving? He rubbed his chin with his bony fingers, listening patiently but wearily. Nothing I said seemed to shock or interest him. I kept talking, my underarms dampened with sweat.

"That's enough." He aimed his gold-tipped pen at the screen. "I understand the situation."

"Help me, please. I don't have much time."

His distant, sympathetic gaze traveled down my body, then back up. "I know."

"I'll pray every night for your help." I said this too hurriedly; it made me sound insincere.

"You shouldn't be ashamed," he said when I wrapped the

robe tightly around me. "You're a beautiful woman. A woman's body is one of God's most beautiful creations."

I watched his interest lift and fall. Lift, fall. I didn't know how to read him.

One day we were lined up in the corridor, arms raised above our heads and legs fanned out, toes touching the toes of the next person. Our bodies merged into one as the *ajumma*'s hand traveled up our robes. It moved vigilantly across every part of our bodies, looking for a weapon. How different my life had become: so specific, so small.

"A set of chopsticks has disappeared," said the madam. "Before you hurt yourself and create a mess for others, you may as well turn it in." She marched up and down past the dozen of us.

Utensils disappeared, so we began eating rice and kimchi with our hands and drank our soup straight from plastic bowls. Sometimes a piece of kimchi or a spoonful of savory *dwenjang* helped me escape. One bite, and I was back at home, in my village, past the checkpoint and through the concrete walls surrounding our grid of houses. It was winter, and the walls were heavy with drifts of glittering snow. My nose burned from the cold, but there was a fire going in Eomma's kitchen. I was finally safe, near the warming flames. As Eomma stirred a pot over the burning *agungi,* making bean curd to sell at the market, I touched her broad back.

Eomma, I said, I'm finally home. Eomma turned and I saw that it wasn't her at all, but a man from the Ministry of People's Security in my *eomma*'s navy dress who struck me on the head with the boiling cast-iron pot.

But I wasn't daydreaming anymore. My dark dreams were real, the pain was real, and I was struck, and struck again.

The two black suits in my room moved with grace for such large men. One of them knocked aside my tray. Stew splattered and dried anchovies scattered across the floor. I backed away against the bedpost; there was nowhere to go. They didn't hurry. I begged; it didn't help. The hand that slapped me across the head came down so slowly; the pain wasn't as bad as the waiting.

"Save me?" said one man. One of his eyes was welded shut and his knuckles were tattooed with Han characters.

My plans had been discovered.

"Some guy's offered to buy you and any others from your country. What have you been saying to our customers?"

Something was about to change. The snowdrifts blocked me in, and I shivered in the cold.

15

Danny

The week waiting for Missionary Kwon brought out the worst in us. Gwangsu began talking to himself about escape, Cheolmin started kicking Gwangsu in the shins, Yongju ground his teeth while sleeping, and Bakjun began masturbating all night without bothering to take it somewhere more private, or at least it seemed that way to me each time he interrupted my sleep. Only Namil was unaffected, as long as he got three square meals a day. I waited for a chance to use Missionary Lee's cell phone or for Missionary Kwon to expel me for challenging him in front of the Bangs—whichever came first. If anyone could help my friends, it was my mom—I just needed to reach her.

The day Missionary Kwon returned, Namil was napping on the floor as stiff as a mummy, the Bible spread over his eyes; Bakjun was staring down at the words as if they were Egyptian hieroglyphs. While I drew Bible scenes on cardboard cards for them, Cheolmin ran back and forth across the room, slamming his body into the walls. He halted and screamed, "There's a hole in my stomach! I can't take it!" then ran again.

"You can, you can and you will." Yongju stopped recopying the Book of Isaiah into a notebook. "We have to."

Missionary Lee wiped at the sweat beading on his forehead and upper lip. "It's Missionary Kwon's orders. I'm sorry."

He had banished Cheolmin from lunch for the second time that week for not memorizing his daily Bible verse.

"He won't know if you let me eat or if I piss in my pants, since he's never around."

"I made a promise. It's my duty." Missionary Lee looked fatigued. "And if you keep using such language, I won't have a choice but to report you."

"He's never been to school, so how can he read?" Bakjun bit off the skin from his thumb. Of course he was also talking about himself. "And now he has to memorize the Bible?"

Memorize wasn't exactly the right word for it. In the missionaries' defense, outside of the daily Bible verse the boys were assigned, they weren't expected to know much more than the Bible's stories in the right order. But it was a strange new world for them, even if the version we were reading was in their Joseon language and not the Korean two cousins removed that was spoken in South Korea. Seeing it through their eyes, it had become strange for me, too. I wondered about the mysterious ways of God and about how long you could keep a group of teenage guys locked up without consequences.

Namil said, "Do you always have to do what Kwon wants you to?"

"All promises are a promise to God." Missionary Lee clapped his hands together and brightened. "How about some snacks? I can do that."

The rare treat went wrong when Cheolmin grabbed the last Choco Pie and knocked over Bakjun's bottle of Coke. I set it upright in a flash, but a quarter of it had spilled, and everyone scrambled to rescue their notebooks and Bibles.

"You stupid *ganna saekki*." Bakjun kept his voice low so it wouldn't carry to Missionary Lee's room, where he was resting. He was always resting those days, which should have been a sign. "That was mine! When do we ever get to drink this stuff?"

Bakjun was sweeping the spilled liquid into his palm when Cheolmin smashed the crown of his head with his elbow.

I locked Cheolmin's arms behind him the best I could. I wasn't about to push my luck with a guy who'd begun talking about returning to his country and joining a legendary gang.

Bakjun's eyes narrowed into flints. The tension in the air scared me; for the first time I sensed that in the confined space, there was nowhere for their energy to go. I released Cheolmin and sprinted to the middle of the room, threw my arms wide, and said the first thing I could think of.

"Once upon a time it was the darkest night ever imagined. God dipped his hand into that darkness and when he opened his arms"—I spread mine out—"he divided the dark from the light."

"This is stupid," said Cheolmin.

"Listen to Daehan," said Yongju. "You two can have my Coke and Choco Pie."

"The light was as bright as the white in a burning fire, a

dove's wing, the streak of a missile across the sky. That was how bright it was."

I described Adam as he wandered through the unruly topiary of nature and showed them how lovely he was, how innocent. Soon enough I was there with Adam and Eve, strolling through Eden, the sting of orchids thick in my nose, the green foliage wrapped around the trees like a sarong, listening to the larks and nightingales. I admired those fateful apples, so luminous that they reflected Adam back to himself like a mirror. I was singing one of the greatest songs that man has ever known, and I was flooded with love and hope. But whether that love was for the story, for comfort, or for faith, I didn't know anymore. I continued until the fate of the world's first man and woman unraveled and the end came: "Dust you are, dust you will return."

I opened my eyes. No one had moved.

"It's not a bad story, when you say it that way." Bakjun cuffed me on the head, sending happy tingles through me.

"I've never heard a nightingale sing," said Yongju. "I like the sound of it. Nightingale."

Cheolmin spat into the air and caught the descending blob in his fist. "Those Bible stories are a load of shit. Everyone knows that."

"Everyone?" I said. "Have you talked to the entire world's population and checked? Do you have any idea how many of us have infiltrated the planet? In China alone there are more than two billion homo sapiens wreaking havoc . . ."

"There he goes, acting like he's intellectual when he's just a homeless Joseon-*jok*. There's easier ways to get out." Cheolmin flashed both palms covered with tiny drawings at me, his version of crib notes.

Namil slung an arm around me, so close that his unwashed hair trailed its oiliness across my cheek. "At least he knows something. At least he's saying something worth listening to."

"And where'd your fancy long words and your fancy learning get you, *dongmu*?" said Cheolmin. "Here, with us."

I slung my arm over Namil's shoulder. "I enjoy learning."

"'I enjoy learning,'" Cheolmin parroted back in a squeaky voice that sounded nothing like mine. My stomach tightened. I was exposed again in a circle of boys and there was nowhere to hide. I prepared myself, curled up roly-poly on the floor to protect myself from his fists, but they never came.

Instead, Yongju asked, "Who's your real enemy? Who are you really angry at?"

He approached Cheolmin gently, like a rustling leaf. "Daehan's one of us, too, and right now we're all we have."

No one had ever defended me before; no one had ever been on my side. I was touched; I was speechless.

Maybe my life would have spun out differently if Yongju hadn't crouched on the floor and put his arm around my shoulders and one around Cheolmin's. But he pulled me into his musk and amber, drew me into the secret fraternity of men, until I was drowning in the oceanic span of his long arms, finally lost.

I hadn't recovered when Missionary Kwon arrived later that afternoon; maybe I have never recovered. He cleared his throat, his eyes resting on Cheolmin, who was sleeping facedown on the *dojjari.* I was teaching Namil how to do a handstand, and he tumbled to the floor feet first as I let go of him and sprang to eager attention, hands at my sides. I'd be more useful to them on the outside anyway, I told myself. I wanted to leave immediately, even if it meant facing my parents.

I could have timed Missionary Kwon's steps toward Cheolmin with a metronome. He inspected him, then disappeared down the hall and returned with Missionary Lee.

"Is this how you're running my safe house?" Missionary Kwon's quiet voice could have needled straight through a bolt of wool.

"We were just taking a break." Missionary Lee frantically shook Cheolmin by the shoulders.

Missionary Kwon pulled up Cheolmin by his armpits and held him like a scarecrow. Missionary Lee did nothing. Cheolmin grabbed Missionary Kwon's hands and dug in with his nails, his face screwed up with so much fury that I ducked as if his fists were flying at me.

"You could have hurt him!" said Missionary Lee, but he stayed half-hidden behind Yongju.

Still holding him by the armpits, Missionary Kwon lifted Cheolmin into the air until their faces were inches apart. "I hear you haven't been very successful in memorizing your daily verses."

"He's only missed a few, and he's really trying," said Missionary Lee.

"Missionary Kwon, I am trying." Cheolmin's eyes were hard and cold.

The missionary set him back down.

"No dinner today for you. No verse, no food. We'll stick to

this every day until you conform fully to my rules. I'll come personally to check if I have to, but I expect . . ."

He frowned, drawing out the fine lines under his eyes. "I expect Missionary Lee will be honest in his reports."

Cheolmin said, "You heard. I tried. I got most of it."

"Most? If the Lord's sacrifice of his own son saved us from most but not all of our sins, would that be enough to bless us with the eternal gift of heaven?"

"And if I give up? Are you going to starve me?" The bulldog look came over Cheolmin's face.

"No, don't try blackmailing me. I don't recommend that. One girl I tried to help—she went on a sort of strike. She wouldn't study or read the Lord's words—she abandoned her soul. I can tell you we were patient, and we moved her from safe house to safe house for more than three years."

A chorus of voices, including mine, said, "Three years?"

"We tried so hard not to give up on her . . . The discipline's for your sake, *jaashik*. You North Koreans can't understand our system, but trust me, I've done this work for years. Without discipline, this house would be utter chaos. Most Christians won't even take kids like you in, because of the potential trouble."

"They're good boys." Missionary Lee approached Cheolmin and wrapped his arms around his neck. "They're God's children, too!"

Ignoring him, Missionary Kwon turned to me. "I need a word with you, Daehan. That shouldn't surprise you." I was ready.

I followed him down the exposed concrete stairs and out the front gate toward his car, my head a muddle. Who I was, what I believed, all the neat black-and-white boundaries of the map of my life no longer made sense. I rubbed at my hair, my cheeks, and wished I could strip out of my skin. The sun warmed my back after precisely ninety-nine days without direct sunlight on it and the foothills were finally a verdant green, but none of it mattered.

He dusted off the boxy sedan's windshield and windows with a soft mop from the trunk, taking his time. I waited a few steps behind him, my hands folded together. I realized that my ankles were peeking out from my pants, and that in the last months I'd outgrown Missionary Kwon. He got into the car and fiddled with the navigation system, then looked out at me. "Are you going to stand there all day?"

So I lowered myself onto the hot prickle of the passenger seat, prepared to be kicked out of the safe house and be liberated.

He tapped impatiently at the black screen. "Do you know how to make this work?"

Of course I understood the psychology of machines, which was actually only the psychology of their maker. I watched Missionary Kwon from the corner of my eye, the smooth facade of his face, which was beginning to remind me of a salesman's. What he'd said about discipline and faith in the safe house was probably mostly true, but it was also unjust and cruel and, worst of all, dangerous. I was thinking about the nature of God, and especially about how to confess, when Missionary Kwon started the car and I was suddenly off the premises with a man I'd accused of being a potential murderer.

I prepared myself. "Missionary Kwon—"

"Daehan, I want to tell you a story about a man," he said. "This man is me."

Before I could stop him, he launched into how he had once languished in a South Korean jail, a no-good man abandoned by society. I became extremely uncomfortable, suffocated as I was by my own secrets.

"I lost everyone—my wife, my brothers and sisters—to my ways. I lost my son."

He tapped a photo dangling from the rearview mirror, a grave young boy around six. I couldn't imagine Missionary Kwon as a father, but then maybe no one ever really seemed like a father.

"There wasn't anything illegal I didn't do. I did my time as a loan shark, I ran a gambling ring, I had my hand in everything until I got caught. My son would be your age now, you know. He's in Cheonan, in South Korea. I get to see him a few times a year. That's it. If I show up at any other time, my wife calls the police. The church saved me. God tested me, and I tested him, but now I know he reserved me for a greater purpose."

My North Korean friends, and the others before him, were the greater purpose.

I asked, "Why are you telling me this?"

He kept talking as if he were speaking more to himself than to me. I managed to stay quiet the way an older man would expect me to and kept my eyes fixed on that dangling family photo. My head was filled with his confessions, this family man, the man with a dark underbelly of a past, who helped and hurt the people entrusted to him. A man, in the end, who believed in God.

Finally, we stopped near the river, a very different river in the summer heat with its banks overgrown with willow trees. There were smugglers openly working in some sort of cooperation with a border guard, sending their goods across with a car tire supporting a length of plywood. The village on the other side had gray walls surrounding peaked roofs and chimneys. Men were fishing, a woman was doing laundry in the river, and kids were playing on the bank. It seemed so safe, bucolic even.

"Missionary Kwon—"

"Pay attention. I drove here for you." He lowered the windows. "*Geogi*, there're journalists in that car ahead. Probably South Korean. There they are."

They were filming the fishermen across the river. The North Koreans, finally noticing the camera's body jutting out of the tinted window, wearily thrust their fishing rods in the air as if they were used to being watched. Only one of the men threw his rod to the ground. The camera panned across them. It was as if a whole society was being watched and followed against its will. I wanted to throw rocks at the reporters in their cars and stop them.

"We shouldn't be gawking at them," I said. "They're people."

"Half of those kids'll probably cross over as soon as the water warms up a little; they'll beg and make some money for their family or keep eating whatever they find until they're full or get caught. Most of them only care about food. You'd be that way, too, if you'd been hungry your whole life. I make it my business to know as many of the kids who cross as I can."

"You were looking for North Koreans the first day we met." I recalled his disappointment when I told him I was a Joseon-*jok*. "Actually, that day—"

"You ever thought about what happens to them after crossing? They take on a new identity and name. They invent a biography for themselves—at least until they have to be more truthful so that someone like me can double-check their story and give them shelter. If they're ever lucky enough to cross into a third country, most reinvent themselves all over again. But they'll always be North Korean. The way they talk and think, the things they know and the things they don't, their history wiped out in a new country—it marks them forever. They go to South Korea with their fantasies and are ashamed when they're looked down at, or shocked when people suspect them of being spies, or act wary, or, worse, stop caring. I've seen it hundreds of times. They don't have a choice, you see. Unlike you."

My head snapped up.

"All this time, I believed you were an orphan, like me. How long were you going to continue with that story?"

He pulled a leaflet out of his jacket pocket and showed me the Chinese and Korean printing announcing a missing son, an image of myself mugging for the camera in a T-shirt printed with a bearded Leo Tolstoy. My palms became clammy.

He ripped up the flyer and let the two halves of my face flutter to his feet.

"I'm a man chosen by God to serve him, and by making a fool out of me, you've made a fool out of God."

I anticipated, even hoped for, a slap across the face. He only flicked up his hand to check his watch.

The wind gusted in through the car windows, then stilled. It was as if God had come and spoken to us, but we didn't know how to understand him. I felt the weight of what I'd put my parents through, my fear of facing them, and loneliness, the trough of turbulent feelings and fears that I couldn't share with anyone.

I buried my face in my hands. "I'll pack my things when we get back."

"Where do you think you're going?"

My head jerked up. "Aren't you going to send me away?"

"Not until we move everyone out. It's for everyone's safety. We can't let you out now that you know where the house is."

"So I can't leave?"

I was still digesting this when he handed me a cell phone, one he used for general phone calls. I called my dad, as the missionary had instructed, and, because I had no choice, let my *abba* know that I was still safe and that I would be home soon enough.

That night I rolled closer to Yongju's back than before, until we were touching. With my chin against the braid of his backbone, I felt the rise and fall of his breathing. My body's heat must have been comforting, for he didn't retreat. I lay there trying not to think about anything, when his shoulders began to shake and I realized he was crying. I didn't know what to do. Shudders continued to move through him.

I raised my hand and ventured to rub his back the way my mom used to do for me when I had the flu. I was electric with feeling. I was afraid of God. The pace of Yongju's breathing slowed until he was asleep, but I stayed alert. How could I sleep, curved so close to his body's fetal position, afraid and grateful, and finally, despite everything, content?

All sorts of black thoughts, and bright thoughts, continued their midnight invasion. I gave up on sleep and escaped to the common room. I didn't know what to do, so I dropped to my knees in front of the hanging cross, closed my eyes, and prepared to embark on a great carpet of prayer for the North Koreans in their country to someday live free from tyranny. I wanted to pray that those responsible for countless crimes against their own people be punished, that the international community be more courageous, and especially that those hiding in China find the freedom they had risked so much for. I wanted to pray for Missionary Lee, for my family, my friends, and especially for myself. But the words wouldn't come.

I got up. I wanted to be near Yongju; I wanted him safe. I did have choices. I finally crept into Missionary Lee's room and began searching. It was easier than I'd thought, since his snoring covered up my small sounds. I moved a foot a minute, it seemed, my hand creeping through his drawers, his shelves, his suitcase pockets. Then I saw the cell phone and the solar charger on the windowsill.

The sky was at its darkest; in a few hours it would be day. From the common room I pressed in my mom's number—the same one she'd had in America—before I lost courage. She might not know who to talk to or might not want to get involved; but with my hand cupped around my mouth, I did what I had to. I called.

16

Yongju

It still hurts to remember how Jangmi was returned to us. When Missionary Kwon had proudly showed me the photos of his new women, I never dreamed Jangmi would be among them. But she was, and I persuaded the missionary to bring her to us. But then she entered behind him with her right foot in a cast and her eyes, dull as lumps of charred coal, gazing out as if there was nothing in the world left to look at. The heaviness she brought with her suffocated all my words. The woman who hovered behind Missionary Kwon like a harnessed ox was Jangmi but not Jangmi. The Jangmi I knew didn't avoid your eyes but looked around defiantly, studying her surroundings and storing up information, the way the hunted do. The Jangmi I knew didn't have a flat stomach.

Questions welled up inside me. What had happened to her? Where had he brought the others from? What had become of my *eomma* and *dongsaeng*? My long hair prickled my neck, my armpits dampened with sweat. It was as if I had suddenly discovered my body. The story of her journey was written on hers: She limped ahead on a walking stick as if the floor was littered with nails. Her right leg was swollen above the plaster; mottled yellowed bruises banded around her forearm and disappeared up the sleeve of her baggy dress.

Daehan dropped the Bible flash cards he was trimming into perfect rectangles, scattering them like paper rain. His finger pointing at her was as straight as an arrow. "You're the one who stole from us!"

He surged ahead with accusations, but it was as if she couldn't hear him, couldn't see any of it: the *saang* we ate on that wobbled on its fourth leg, the stacks of *banseok* we sat on to cushion the floor, the bookshelf lined with black Bibles and hymnals, our names branded on them. The others and me.

Gwangsu got up so quickly that he fell and hit his head on the *saang*.

"Pretty *nuna*." Cheolmin's voice was so sharp it could have honed knives. "When was the last time we saw you? Oh, I remember! When you betrayed us!"

"What's she doing here?" Bakjun chimed in.

"Keep your mouths shut," Missionary Kwon said. "Thanks to Jangmi, I was able to help a number of other girls to my shelters, but she needed special attention—medical attention." He meant the Christian doctor he trusted who lived in the area.

Her solitude was impenetrable; she didn't once look at Missionary Kwon during this speech or when he told Missionary Lee, "It was one of our most expensive rescue missions."

Cheolmin looked as if he would take her apart piece by

piece with his jagged teeth. "So there's enough money to pay for a load of women, but not enough to get us out of China?"

"Look here," I said. "She's one of us. She needed help. That's what matters."

Cheolmin snorted, all residual respect for my age and status, all hope, gone. Only Namil smiled at Jangmi, showing the threads of lunch's blanched spinach trapped between his teeth, then shrugged his shoulders.

"She's bad news," Daehan pronounced in my ear, his voice full of worry. "You shouldn't get involved in her affairs."

While the boys complained, Missionary Lee spread his arms like an eagle and gave her an awkward hug, surrounding her small frame. She shuddered and pressed back into the bookcase so hard that its skeleton must have imprinted itself on her back. No corner seemed deep enough for her.

"I'm so sorry," Missionary Lee stammered, and he clumsily dusted off her shoulders, her stomach, as if trying to brush away his fingerprints. She let out a small, raking scream at his touch, and I could only guess what must have happened to her.

Missionary Lee said, "Is there something you want, my child? Is there anything I can do for you at all? Maybe some food?" His voice squeaked with alarm.

She looked away. "I want to be without this body. I want to be air. Can you make that happen?"

Missionary Kwon thumped the wall and addressed the boys. "I demand obedience. Who runs this house? Who gives the orders here? She is staying because I said she's staying."

I promised to watch over her, and Missionary Kwon knew I

kept my word. My words—I was embarrassed for those helpless, fluttering birds as adrift as I was.

Once Missionary Kwon left, the others bowed together in a conspiratorial circle, touching.

After Jangmi had fled our mountain dugout, questions made fierce revolutions in my head. Now more questions. What had happened to her? Did I really care about her, about anyone, or were my expressions of interest merely a way of escaping myself? One thing was certain: No doctor could repair what was broken inside Jangmi.

All afternoon, while she rested, I glued and painted the wood crosses that Missionary Kwon had us make for churches located overseas. I worked slowly, deliberately. There were so many fraught elements involved, and my own considerations daunted me. I saw walls that I shouldn't broach: a *nuna* four years my senior who was once with child, my desire in search of an object.

"She's dangerous," said Daehan, his words as wild as weeds. "Someone who's stolen and betrayed us will do it again."

He wasn't wrong. But she had done it for her child. I said like a fool, "I can be betrayed again."

"Sympathy is healthy. Sympathy I get." His eyes darkened. "But someone like her couldn't possibly be interesting to you."

He meant an uneducated, provincial woman, an *ajumma* knowledgeable in the womanly ways, all stories I had already told myself.

His words provoked me. I chopped fresh ginger the way my *eomeoni* had once done for me and made her tea. As I walked to

Jangmi's room, a mighty hand seemed to seize a gun's barrel and aim it at my chest. I saw the red leather jacket. The women I loved, their feet knocked against the ground like hollowed-out gourds as they were dragged away. I halted at the door's threshold, memories lodged in my throat like a curved fish bone.

July had turned the building into a greenhouse of trapped stale air, but Jangmi was balled up under a blanket, her arms shielding her head. As if I even knew how to be dangerous.

As soon as I set the tray beside her, she flung the blanket away. The room tipped for me as her eyes touched mine. The melancholy of her eyes. They felt like home. She didn't belong to the acidic stink of waste and urine seeping out of the bathroom and the brassy smell of our bodies in the boarded-up heat that made you gag if you breathed too deeply. The sole of her foot was as tough as animal hide, but her toes were somehow still perfectly formed, like cultured pearls. It moved me, her rough elegance.

"What do you want? I don't have anything to give you and you don't have anything I need."

She was so direct, so different from Myeonghui, who already felt like another life.

"Why do you think I want something?"

"Everyone wants something from each other."

She wasn't wrong, but I said, "I want to stay right here."

"Why?" She shook her head. "I'm capable of much, much worse."

She grabbed my knee, digging in. "Tell me, *dongmu,* what would you do to get out of this country? Would you kill, if you had to?"

She raised those words to her lips so easily.

I thought about the Dear Leader, the man in the red leather jacket. "Not everyone deserves to live."

"No, maybe they don't."

I said, "You, *dongmu,* would you?"

She told me to sit beside her, so I did. I would have done anything she told me to. My fingers tingled when she took my hands in hers.

"You have such pretty hands." Her smile was turbulent. "I've never seen such beautiful hands. Maybe hands like yours aren't made for killing."

I thought about my *eomeoni,* pushed into a van. My sister, how they had lifted her up when she wouldn't quiet down and dropped her into the van like a chopped-down tree. How I couldn't do anything for them.

"You can do anything." I gazed at her. "You're stronger than I am."

It was Daehan who told me we were organisms of infinite hunger, born hungry infants before we are able to form permanent memories. There were as many different kinds of hunger as there were people. Change and stillness, love and solitude, freedom and tyranny, all of them to me were synonyms for hunger. To be beyond hunger, I thought, must be a place beyond desire.

A colony of parasites nested inside Jangmi. She ate bowls of rice, soybean-paste stew, spicy pork when it was available, as if eating would stave off thinking. I began giving her half my portion; she reminded me of what it meant to be hungry.

On the fourth day I set the dinner tray beside her and lit her a candle, as had become my routine. She eyed me, a potential predator. "You're wasting your time being nice. You're not getting anything from me."

"It's for myself," I said. She looked as if nothing I said could make her believe me.

Her hands clutched at the blanket and the veins rose on the backs of her hands. "I don't need friends. I've always taken care of myself."

"Think of me as a *dongsaeng,* not as a man. I can be a little brother. I can be anyone now."

"*Dongsaeng?*" She shrugged. "It's been a long time since I've had anything like a *dongsaeng.*"

We couldn't eat ice cream or thrill ourselves with amusement park rides, try foreign foods like hamburgers and pretend to enjoy them, or walk by the river the way I had with Myeonghui. We couldn't do anything. But we were usually together.

She told me about her few happy childhood moments, how she wished she'd been born a man because men lived free from fear. I painted a village for her on the wall, the sky a cerulean blue, a sun glowing with heat and light. When she limped out on her walking stick for the first time, hope grew in me. But after one look at Cheolmin's and Bakjun's prowling eyes, at Daehan's stormy eyebrows, she rushed back into her concrete box.

I ate quickly and went to her with a tray.

"There wasn't enough room at the *saang,*" she said.

While she ate, I tried to read the Bible. The words of Daniel walked in front of me. One tiny black leg of each letter ahead of the next, then the next. The ㄷ wiggled ahead of the ㅅ. The 이 slowly clambered over the 한. When I woke up, there was a pillow under my head—Jangmi's.

I sat upright. Imagined her hands cradling my head, my neck. "Do you want your pillow back?"

"What pillow?" she said scornfully.

We sat in silence. Suddenly she laughed, and her hands fluttered up and covered her mouth. Her laugh, her gesture, moved through me as real and necessary as water or sleep.

"You're a good person," she said. She sounded surprised by herself. Then she leaned in and I smelled the sweet sesame of her breath. "My baby—she never even had a name."

Soon we had a second intruder, a white man who Missionary Kwon called an ally of our people. Still, we shrank from the tall American who ducked to pass through the front door. I assumed all white people were Americans. The man had a thin, ungenerous nose and an overdeveloped torso, like a tree stump. He took off his black cap and sunglasses and said, "I've been so eager to meet all of you."

His eyes were the color of grass. He wasn't my first white man; there were times in Pyongyang when people parted at a white man's approach, afraid to attract attention by looking at him, and I'd seen plenty of them in smuggled movies.

"Say hello to our guest." There was a warning in Missionary Kwon's voice.

The man's broad smile didn't drop away and he waved both

hands in the air to show that he was harmless. But he was a stranger and a foreigner, and only Daehan and I managed to greet him in formal Korean.

The white man addressed us with the honorific form in pristine Korean and bowed, confusing us. We were young, we were refugees—used to pity but never respect—we were the ones who should be bowing. I found myself bowing back, a situation so absurd that I laughed. But this only angered me. Laughing, when everyone I loved was gone.

All around me the murmurs began. "White man, white man."

"Matthew's an American raised in South Korea. He's an ally of yours—a friend." As usual, Missionary Kwon gave us a skeletal explanation. "I expect you to tell him all about your lives and answer his questions."

"I'm not eating at a table with a long-nose," Bakjun said, standing to his full height, at age sixteen no bigger than ten-year-olds I would see in the South.

"Nonsense." Missionary Kwon was firm. The American was a journalist and the son of Missionary Kwon's good friend. "Matthew's father came as a missionary himself to South Korea several decades ago and is now one of the country's best pastors. His family's practically Korean."

This man drew back at the mention of his father.

"Too good," he said in perfect Korean, and laughed hoarsely. "He's a hard man to live up to." It hurt to think that I could never be a better son for my *abeoji*.

The stranger's head tilted toward each of us as he presented himself as a friend to all. He bowed awkwardly in every direction, his sloppy smile spilling into the room. But he, like everyone else in China, wanted something from us.

That night, terse fragments drifted out from Missionary Lee's room.

"A white man, and a journalist!" said Missionary Lee sharply, and he was never sharp. "That's dangerous, dangerous for all . . . He'll be all over their lives—they've been . . . he could expose them. We're here to do God's work, not to sell stories."

"Part of the Lord's work is letting people know what's happening in that dark country," said Missionary Kwon. "Matthew will live here, no one will see him; he's going to write . . . and with the donations we'll have coming in . . ."

"There's enough money."

"You know nothing." Missionary Kwon's voice rose, but only a little. "Where's the windfall going to . . . The sky? The trees? Trees don't pay for my shelters."

"God, God will provide," Missionary Lee said. "If we don't believe that, what do we have?"

Missionary Kwon wasn't present the next morning. Neither was Missionary Lee, who felt ill and stayed in bed. There was only this Matthew.

The journalist Matthew was deft—too deft—at handling our suspicion and unease and the sneaking stares at the light brown fuzz, like that of a deer's antlers, that seemed to cover every part of him. He called it his animal hair, tugging at a crinkly strand as he smiled. None of it unnerved him.

He waited. He ate our food with exaggerated relish, popping a spicy strand of kimchi into his mouth at breakfast as if to show us: *I'm like you.* He regaled us with stories about being a white man in Asia, though the boys probably only listened so they could skip studying. He passed out exotic sweets and played soccer with them, impressing Namil by keeping the deflated ball aloft for more than a hundred kicks, bouncing it from ankle to knee to hip to head. It wasn't hard to like him. Only later did he maneuver us to the storage room, one at a time, and, wedged between the sacks of beans and cans of ham, retrieve our stories from us.

When it was my turn, he cajoled and waited as I fled, avoided him, then reluctantly returned. He was armed with Missionary Kwon's directive: Ask them anything you want, anything. He knew how to be patient; he sympathized, he prodded with his florid language. To tell was to remember and to remember was to relive, but I had little choice. I cooperated. We all did, except for Jangmi, who refused to be interviewed.

We sat in a messy circle with Matthew on his last afternoon, waiting for the dipping creak of the front door, the particular music of Missionary Kwon's arrival. Matthew massaged the pocket stitching of his slacks and said to us, but really to Jangmi, "I was the only white person in a class of forty-five South Korean high schoolers. You been to high school?" He continued. "Mine was on Jeju Island! You ever heard of Jeju Island?"

He told her about the place, an island surrounded by azure sea, full of lava tubes and sunflowers, with a dormant volcano in the middle. South Koreans had always honeymooned there, though the well-off now headed to Europe or to tropical countries. He glanced down the hall. He must have known that the missionaries didn't like South Korea spoken of around us because they said it made us restless. "Where did you grow up? Was it beautiful there, too?"

A tremor passed through her as if her past was moving through her and taking hold, demanding payment.

"I know it's difficult for you. I won't use your name or your face. Your story's important—it's the only way to stop the abuses you've suffered in China from happening."

That may have been true, but Jangmi wasn't ready to speak.

"Nothing happened to me," she said. "I crossed a river and lived in a room. And now I live in another room."

The journalist crouched close to her, his green eyes turning filmy in the reflected light. "Missionary Kwon told me where he found you. It must be so hard. Let me help you."

Though he was my senior in all ways, I set my hand down on the journalist's shoulder so that he couldn't lean in any closer to Jangmi. "Can't you see she doesn't want to talk to you?"

Matthew raised his arms high into the air. "Look, I'm a good guy, really."

She sought my other hand, laying hers lightly across mine.

"Do people like me get to go to your country?" Her question made even Cheolmin freeze.

"My country?" Matthew smiled. "If you mean America, actually, yes," he said, his voice lowered. "Once you're out of China, you can apply to live in a number of different countries. Japan, Norway, South Korea, America, you name it. It's called asylum."

"You know people, important people," she said. "If you

wanted to, you could help us. The longer we're in China, the more dangerous it is for us. You know that."

He stood up. "I'm just a journalist, not a diplomat."

Jangmi let go of me and gripped his ankle.

"Help me get out," she whispered. "I'm begging. You have the power."

He shielded his eyes. "You need to stop this."

"If you help me, you can take as many photos as you want and I'll tell you everything you would ever want to know." Her fingers turned white as she strengthened her grip. "Things you can't even imagine."

He looked awkward and afraid. "Missionary Kwon knows best what to do."

The light and speed went out of her. "He'll keep us as long as he can. Kids? A woman, a boy from Pyongyang? We're his prizes."

"She's right," I said. "But you're different from them—the Christians."

Matthew shook his head vigorously. "Believe me, there are many different kinds of Christians."

Jangmi said, "We didn't risk our lives just to end up in this jail. There's no one in this room who crossed without thinking they could die. You must be able to help us—you know people."

"I don't, it's not like you think." He pried her fingers from his ankle and backed away. "I trust Missionary Kwon knows what he's doing. Give him time."

That night, I dreamed that people were after me. I was wading through the river again, half-naked and shivering in its glassy chill. I was in Pyongyang watching a Hollywood movie with a friend: I was Leonardo DiCaprio, I was Tom Cruise. Now I was sleeping on cold, marbled rock. Pine needles jabbed into my back.

I woke up and a cool hand brushed across my sweaty forehead. A familiar voice said, Wake up, my son. It was my *eomeoni,* so I followed her. We journeyed in reverse across the river and the barren mountains of our country, and back to our home in Pyongyang. The house invited and repelled, opened and closed. It opened again, and we were inside, gazing at another family's belongings: old-fashioned celadon vases showcased in the hall, a set of painted ceramic dolls, the portraits of our leaders dusted and prominently displayed in gold frames. No one was back from work or school and still the house echoed with bright, new voices. I felt betrayed.

"And look here," Eomeoni said, and we were suddenly outside a mansion barricaded by gate upon gate. Tanks surrounded the perimeter, their great noses pivoting toward us until we were past the first gold-plated gate, past a golf course and ponds, a riding stable and a verdant forest with families of deer, then finally inside, under the light of a heavy chandelier.

"Look." Eomeoni withdrew a gun from her sable coat. "Here is where your father died."

I wasn't ready to die yet, so I left her and walked out.

I was walking in the dream in which I had awakened from a dream, and then I was only walking. I found myself in the common room, in its great white silence. The full moon seemed to step on my foot's shadow. Twice I whirled around, but there was no one there, just the sensation of breath, the weight of heavy steps that seemed to pursue me.

I went to check on Jangmi, hesitating before looking in. Blankets were pushed into a corner in the shape of a body. The moonlight caught silver cobwebs tangled across the corners of the walls, dust rustled across the room, and there was Jangmi. Jangmi, on the ledge of the window whose plastic sheath she had sliced open with the kitchen scissors, her plastered leg already swung over the ledge, and the other tucked up to her chest, as she breathed in the night air. Her hair flamed blue in the moonlight. She looked peaceful, almost—happy. But her breath came in raspy huffs, as if someone were choking her. She swung the other leg over.

I stepped slowly across the gritty floor, dizzy, the room devouring me. She was so close—if only I could convince her to wait out the masquerade of the days and months until we were finally free to make the dangerous journey to a safe third country. Then one of her legs settled on the other side of the sill; for her there must have only been the reality of the ledge.

There was a hot hiss of liquid, and a musky smell rose from her. I caught a glimpse of her wet, trembling leg. She was afraid, of course she was afraid to jump. If I made a mistake, one more life would be lost.

"*Dongmu.*" I kept my voice a gentle harmony even as my heart thundered in my ears. "Take my hand. You've gotten this far."

"You don't know what's happened to me. You're a man . . . you can't know . . ."

I thought of my *eomeoni,* my *dongsaeng,* and it hurt to breathe.

"It's two floors up. You'll be badly hurt, and you won't get what you want."

She made small, shuddering animal pants. The shadows of trees danced across the walls and the wind breathed out, breathed in. Her foot, hands, and lips, her whole body was soaked blue with moonlight. A breeze gusted in, stilled.

"*Dongmu,* trust me."

"Trust is what dead people do." She sucked on a strand of hair caught on her lip. "I want to decide when I die."

"You'll make it out of here, I promise." Slowly, I stepped closer. "We'll make a way."

In that room where time had slowed down, I finally took her by the waist and pulled her trembling body in.

"Just a little more, you're almost there. China's the worst part—everyone says that. We will get out," I said. "We will."

17

Jangmi

Voices whirled outside my room, making shapes that I couldn't understand. The tin sheet of roof rattled with rain. I thought of calling out, suddenly scared of what I might do alone. I didn't trust myself anymore. I gazed at the torn window covering, the great gap into the rest of the world, and I tried to believe that the future still meant something.

This was what I believed: Men are animals. Everybody wants something from one another. Everything is an exchange.

I asked myself: What does Yongju want from me? The missionaries continued to talk. I tried and failed to sleep. Their sounds continued from down the hall as I felt my limbs, my hair against my shoulders. I was all there. My leg smelled of dried urine and my face was tight with dried tears. I disappointed myself. I expected to be stronger than this, for hadn't I given up my world for another?

I heard Missionary Lee say, "Yongju's right. This isn't working. If he hadn't seen her—we almost lost her."

"Who decides what's going to work or not? It takes time."

"The journalist was . . . a mistake."

Their voices continued to drift in. Beside me was a basin of water and a cloth. Yongju had left it for me, and the thought made me feel like a dried-up apple. He had seen me so compromised. I washed my face, then scrubbed down my leg, though someone had already cleaned me up.

Missionary Kwon said, "We're giving them an incredible chance to walk hand in hand in a new life with God. You think the streets are better for them?"

I was so tired. Missionary Lee's voice dropped.

"You don't think I care?" Missionary Kwon asked. "I used to guide them, dodging police, slave traders, border guards. And you're telling *me* that we should send them all south right away because one girl tried to jump?"

"You've devoted your life to helping them," Missionary Lee said. There was some mumbling, then, "We almost lost her."

"What about their religious education? Saving their souls? You know the conversion rates drop steeply once they leave China." There was pacing. "And who will sponsor us if we bring them in for a week or two, then let them go? Which church organization is stupid enough to do that? It's safety or nothing!"

"God will provide," said Missionary Lee. "There are good people everywhere, but *good* is too simple a word to describe God. Maybe the more important question to ask ourselves is, Am I living a good life? A worthy life? We should be asking ourselves this right now."

"Isn't that the clearest thing you've ever heard a Christian say?" Daehan's voice startled me.

Daehan was standing just outside the lantern's ring of light, and though his dislike of me was clear, I was grateful not to be alone.

He hunched down to my level and cupped his hand to my ear. "They're talking about you."

"I know."

"I'm only here because Yongju asked me to keep an eye on you."

As the voices continued to rise, he frantically grabbed handfuls of his hair with both hands. He said he'd been told to board up my window but thought I should have fresh air. He talked about reading the stars the way the ancients had and how he wished we could see the stars that would map our way. Then he gripped my hand.

"Don't give up, *nuna*." His voice was as fervent as his grip. "It's a mistake to give up. I promise I'll get us out of here."

Fatigue overwhelmed me. I wondered if my baby would have been like Daehan, always feeling too much. Or calm, like her *abeoji,* who would always have his way.

The murmurs became shouts.

"This is my life's work. Don't waste my time any longer. Get out."

"Listen—"

"Get out. Get out!"

Missionary Lee entered my room and, with a faltering smile, kissed me on the forehead. Then he grimaced, as if a hand had reached in and squeezed his heart, and toppled sideways to the floor. I drew back from his straw-colored flesh; Daehan shouted for help and the others rushed to the missionary's side.

Missionary Lee murmured, "I'm fine, it's just a little dizziness." His breath was shallow, his forehead sticky with sweat.

Daehan said, "He needs a doctor!"

"I'm perfectly fine, no need for the fuss." The missionary rubbed at his chest.

Within minutes I heard the front door open and the stairs echo with footsteps.

My window was sealed with wood, and slivers of light came in through the slats by the time I woke up. I longed for the sun-covered hill of my village, for the way my *eomma* and I peeled hot potatoes in winter. The heat, I told myself, was responsible for how weak I had become. I crawled out from under the blanket, trying to believe that yesterday was merely the past and everything before that even more distant from me. When Yongju leaned toward me, his face as slender as candlelight, I drew back onto the *yo*.

"Have you been sitting here watching me all night?" I was sure of it.

"Only till this morning." He flexed his feet as if they were numb.

"What happened to Missionary Lee?"

His hand brushed gently across my eyelids, closing them. "I don't know, but, *nuna,* I'll be here, if you need me."

"I don't need anyone." I pulled the thin blanket over my head. But I listened for his movements.

When I dared to look out again, Yongju was slouched against the wall, his fingers picking precisely through the Bible's pages as if they were the taut strings of a *gayageum*. But he wasn't reading; his dark eyes were resting on me. I turned away. Caring about someone was another weakness and I couldn't afford to be weak again.

I hobbled out of the room alone, avoiding the arm he offered me. Daehan darted in once I left, as if he had been outside listening.

The briny smell of the common room made me gag. The others were sprawled and tense in the stifling room. Their every sentence concerned what would happen when Missionary Kwon returned and whether they would finally be sent to a safe country. Their tension shocked me awake, and I flipped through some books from the shelf, the words just pictures to me as I thought about the few choices I had left. Until voices rose from talking to shouting, and Cheolmin slapped Gwangsu across the head.

"Get out of my sight," he said. "You make me sick."

Gwangsu cringed and crawled away on his knees.

Bakjun said, "If I don't get out of here, I'm gonna lose my mind. I'm gonna kill someone. Or maybe I'll jump out of the window."

He looked alarmed as he glanced my way, as if he'd forgotten I was there.

They huddled together, speaking in low voices, until Yongju came out.

Yongju said, "What is it?"

Cheolmin stuck a wad of gum under the *saang*. "Nothing, nothing."

"Just waiting for Missionary Kwon," Bakjun said, "like everyone else."

Yongju stopped in front of them and gave them a long look. "Are you boys hiding something from me? Troubles already multiplying."

"Now we're not even allowed to talk?" A tear ran down Cheolmin's cheek before he angrily wiped it away. "What is this place? Missionary Kwon, and now you?"

When Missionary Kwon returned the following day, I took in his rumpled linen trousers and his shoes still caked with mud, and became anxious. Yongju took the garment bag and suitcase from him, then beat the shoes against the door with his free hand.

"You boys been good?"

Cheolmin said, "What else is there to be here?"

Namil said, "Where's Missionary Lee?"

"It was a heart attack, not Missionary Lee's first, it seems. He had to have double bypass surgery. He's very lucky to be alive."

"You mean Missionary Lee isn't coming back?" Yongju dropped the shoes.

"No, probably not. But that tough old snail will be okay.

God was watching out for him." Missionary Kwon patted Yongju on the back. "You could say his heart sent him a stern warning."

"What will happen to us?" Hope flared in Yongju's voice, but I knew better than to hope.

"You'll be moved to new safe houses in the next few weeks where my people can be with you full-time," Missionary Kwon said. "In the meantime I'll be completely available to you here."

In front of me was another safe house, another bare cell of a room. Like a rock, I would be worn down by the wind and the sand in this country that had taken everything from me. I thought of my *eomma*. Maybe she blamed my *abba,* then me, before retreating into a medicated haze. I thought of how easily I had left her, how I could never take that back.

Cheolmin hurled a slipper at the plastic-covered window. "What kind of scam is this?"

"This is my establishment and my rules." Missionary Kwon unlocked the door and swept it open. "If any of you want to leave, anytime, feel free. You're not a prisoner here."

The boys' voices rose in protest, but no one walked out.

The missionary looked fiercely at us. "How do you understand God's will? You can't understand, you merely accept."

The will to live is stronger than hope, and I made my decision before I knew there was a choice to be made. Maybe I would have decided differently if Missionary Lee had been with us.

The day I was to have my cast removed, Missionary Kwon drove me to the doctor's house, an hour's drive away. It was the first Western-style house I had ever seen.

I had visited this confused house that first terrible time, but only now was I able to see it. Missionary Kwon's hand curved around my waist, his touch an electric shock. "Come," he urged, and steered me into the house.

The back room where I'd been treated before was cluttered with reproductions of paintings and souvenirs from the doctor's travels. Travel, something beyond my understanding. The doctor directed a blur of questions at me, then told me to sit on a long raised bed. While he cut open the cast with an angrily buzzing machine, he kept flashing his pink, fleshy gums and gold fillings at me as if a smile could make everything better. I had lost my family, my country, my unborn baby. Where were the smiles in that? I thought of Yongju's face, how it carried its sadness so plainly, how it comforted.

"All this big country," Missionary Kwon said afterward in the car. The wind carried his words out the window into the green hills. "How do you feel?"

"I feel safe with you." My words came automatically. I knew what men needed to hear.

I knew he needed to be needed by us. And we did need him, he who put food on our table every day and had paid for my escape, who decided when we would be allowed to make the last dangerous crossing. But he couldn't bring my baby back. In that sense there was nothing he could give me.

But that wasn't true, either. When he said suddenly, "Your child is with God," I was filled with gratitude.

I asked, "Is that your son?"

He nodded at the photo hanging from the mirror.

"How old is he?"

He smiled briefly. "Only fourteen, and he already speaks better English than I ever did. He's taking English, taekwondo. And he's already a black belt."

"And your wife?"

His eyes lingered on my face, and I felt his interest rise.

"He's with his *eomma* in Seoul. We're no longer married. Let's just say it's a difficult situation."

On the drive back, he stopped in town to pick up a carton of ice cream from a small corner shop. When he got out, his eyes darted left and right as if he was the hunted one.

Once the road became an empty road to nowhere, soybean fields on both sides, he kept glancing my way. His clean, earthy smell reminded me of newly churned farmland. He had desirably pale skin and wasn't a bad-looking man, though he was thick in the waist and had large yellowed teeth. I took stock as I dipped into the carton of mint chocolate chip, its sweetness so bruising that it stung my tongue. Holy men were still men.

Then he said, "I recently got someone to South Korea." As if he knew precisely what to say to me.

"To South Korea."

"Yes, through my people. I'm capable of doing that, and more." He seemed awed by who he had become.

"Why did she get to go?"

He slowed the car. "What makes you think it's a she?"

I considered his hand, that mighty hand that I swore would be the last in the sequence of hands in my life. I wished all those hands to be dismembered, strung up, hung on a laundry line to dry and shrivel in the sun.

Instead I drifted my hand to his thigh, and waited. I did what I had to do to live.

I didn't know then that Daehan had called his mother and that people outside of Missionary Kwon's organization were starting to move and work for us. I was too used to thinking of myself as alone.

It happened the way I expected. The next night Missionary Kwon walked quietly into my room. He was dressed the way he always was, in a dress shirt, jacket, and slacks. The man seemed to sleep in uniform, so determined to preserve this upright image of himself. He had me follow him to the front door, turned the key, and led me outside into the monsoon rains. I ignored the large umbrella he held out and descended the slippery steps, letting the rain cleanse me. The mud sucked at my slippers and water turned my nightdress into a river. I was alert and ready until I smelled the sweetness of my breasts becoming moist with milk, and my weak leg buckled despite the walking stick. He gripped me by the shoulders and helped me into the backseat of the car. Water pooled under me. As he unzipped his slacks, I prepared myself.

"It's a solitary life, a hard life for any man, even a religious man." His face was half in shadow. He tossed his tie over his shoulder. "You seem to understand that about me."

I tried to remember what my former self would have done and said, and let her guide me.

As he undressed me, my teeth began to chatter. The nub of the seat belt dug into my back, and our breathing steamed up the windows.

He said, "For God has consigned all men to disobedience, that he may show his mercy to all."

He prayed for God to forgive his weak flesh as he pulled down my underwear with his thumbs. His mouth tasted of tart tangerines. The car smelled like a wet towel. My other self, my old self who knew how to survive, kept her eyes fixed on the roof of the car above her and thought about how she might benefit from this exchange. Tried to visualize a future. It wasn't me. It wasn't me at all.

But it was me when we walked up the stairs, my arms and legs heavy, my back bruised by the seat-belt buckle. I tried to focus on the present. Left, right, left, right. One mossy step at a time.

Until I saw Yongju pacing across the common room. His slouching shoulders, the delicate outlines of his worry, were excruciating to see.

"I checked on you, *dongmu,* and you weren't there!" He rushed up to me, relief on his face. How did you—"

As he grasped my hands, Missionary Kwon came in and locked the door behind him.

Yongju's breathing became fast and shallow. Or was it mine? I was wet and chilly, but my cheeks flushed with heat.

"There was a medical emergency." Missionary Kwon folded his arms together. "Everything's fine now, so you should go back to your room." His voice stayed even.

"*Dongmu,*" I said, but Yongju didn't stay to listen.

I followed him to the supply room, too anxious to keep a careful distance. I could have touched him if I'd reached out, but I didn't.

"I do what I have to do," I said.

"You don't have to explain."

But I needed him to know what time had done to me. I wanted someone, finally, to know me. "You don't know how it was for us. At the worst of it, my *abba* continued to go to work at the shoe factory though it stopped paying its workers. All the machines were turned off, but he kept going until he died. My *eomma*? She would boil soup thickened with bits of bark and weeds. The doctor had no medicine for her pneumonia. Then she started taking *bbindu* and the *eomma* I knew disappeared."

I watched his bowed head and told him how afraid I had been, traveling across the country in boy's clothes, hiding from train conductors and sneaking across the border and walking for hours to trade and sell the scraps I had. How my father died from the Great Hunger and left us. "One thing sustained me: the dream of leaving. Now it's the only thing I have left."

I had never spoken so much about myself. Fierce, clipped words tumbled out. I was exhausted, but I didn't know what he would say once I stopped speaking.

His head was still bowed, his fists clenched. It made me sad to look at him for too long.

I said, "I hear my *eomma*'s voice in the rain."

What hurt the most was the way he gazed at me: with

understanding. He stepped closer and his lips brushed across my hair. Almost a light kiss, as if a breeze had passed across it. How could he, knowing what he knew. He uncrossed my arms that were tight around my torso and wiped the corners of my eyes. Tears, another weakness. I looked at the other country that he was for me, at his outrageous idealism. At his innocence.

18

Yongju

The oppressive rains that night would be imprinted on my memory. My nose was full of the ripe bouquet of our rank smells and I tried to escape it, attempting to escape from myself.

The windows were misted over, distorting the trees into swollen, distended shapes that swayed in the wind like naked bodies. Rain stippled my perspective, but I thought I saw a human smudge and pressed my face against the plastic. It was Jangmi, kicking up puddles of water with her feet, holding her nightdress up high from the sludge. I was alarmed and amazed that she had somehow freed herself. She hadn't been broken after all, only hoarding her strength. Maybe her mouth was open, drinking the rain. Maybe she was thinking of me. I thought she was alone.

The moment the door opened, I saw Jangmi's wet nightdress reveal her like a clear glass of water. She was soaked, her water-logged skirt hiked up to mid-thigh, and so thin she looked like she might shatter if you held her. But when I saw Missionary Kwon behind her, his granite hand on her hip, I was the one who cracked.

I tried to forget the way Jangmi's nightdress had revealed her. The way Missionary Kwon looked at me as if he were peering through a microscope.

During the next day's morning service I willed myself not to think, to disappear, when we sang the words "As the deer panteth for the water so my heart longeth after you. You alone are my heart's desire and I long to worship you . . ." and then a half hour later, as Missionary Kwon intoned, "It is impossible to please God without faith . . ." But I resented the gleam of his leather shoes set parallel to each other by the door, his scrubbed smell of pine soap. His white collar, his skin pink and glowing with health like a middle-aged baby, when the skin under my arms was red and prickly with heat rash. There was no calm to be found in a woman turned into a pillar of salt. A man's head served on a platter. An ark floating while all of humanity drowned.

When the rest of us sat down for lunch, Cheolmin stood like a soldier and announced, "I couldn't memorize my verse."

Bakjun stood up beside Cheolmin. "I couldn't, either."

Namil raised himself to his knees. "I didn't, either."

Cheolmin and Bakjun looked angry and uncertain, as if this was as far as they had planned their rebellion. They looked at Missionary Kwon.

"All of you?" Missionary Kwon set down his chopsticks. "All three? And the rest of you let this happen? Do the Lord's words mean anything to you? Do you know why you're here and not out on the street?"

"It's August. We've been stuck inside for months." Cheolmin scraped at his cheeks and flicked away the dead skin. "We're living the same day over and over again and nothing's changed. You haven't kept your promises."

"Listen to that rain." Missionary Kwon ran his fingers through his gelled hair in one even, controlled motion. "There's a lesson in that rain. It's a sign, another Noah's ark, God has sent another flood."

"Noah's ark?" Namil frowned, our early lessons already forgotten.

I said, "Who do you think he's cleansing?"

Missionary Kwon stood up and lifted the *saang* high above our heads so that our chopsticks hovered in the air. He had the audacity to look smug. "Today we'll skip lunch together and pray on an empty stomach. It will give you clarity."

We hadn't crossed and risked our lives for this.

I wasn't surprised when Cheolmin punched the air with his fist. "I don't want anything to be clear—I want to eat!" He looked ready to kill. He snatched Missionary Kwon's Bible from his side and hurled it across the room. A thud resounded; the paper tore.

Missionary Kwon gasped, and his hand flew up to protect his heart. "Gwangsu, Daehan, the rest of you, cover the dishes and store the *banchan* in the icebox for now." His voice was trimmed of feeling and he avoided Jangmi and me, as if we didn't exist.

He said, "Thanks to Cheolmin, we'll fast and pray for a few days and begin our relationship with God over again in the right state of mind. For 'Man shall not live by bread alone, but by every word that comes from the mouth of God.'"

He instructed me to take the storeroom's boxes of canned goods to the front door, then began emptying out the kitchen drawers: dumplings freshly rolled for the night's dinner, a tub of kimchi we had seasoned together, a shelf of vegetables and another of fruit, all the cartons of *banchan,* packages of dry noodles. All of it was deposited into large plastic bags that he ordered Daehan to help carry to the car. He said, "There are others who will appreciate this."

"You mean we won't be eating at all, when there's food?" Bakjun's knuckles scrubbed at his face as if to erase himself. He looked confused and hostile and sorry all at once. "All of us, for days?"

Daehan's hand only passed over his face like a fan, and he lugged the heavy sack out, his feet as heavy as flagstones. I didn't move.

When Missionary Kwon had his nose in one of the drawers, Cheolmin spat on the floor and in one swift movement rammed him with his head, pushing Missionary Kwon into the wall. It was as if my wishing had made it happen. Bakjun took the cue and grabbed the missionary by the shirt with two fists. "You liar!"

Cheolmin said, "Come on! We'll get *goryangju* with his money."

Namil and Gwangsu followed as they clamped themselves on the missionary's legs. I could have stopped them, but instead I let them sabotage months of patience. When Jangmi limped in the missionary's direction, I blocked her behind me. I said, "He deserves worse."

"How dare you raise your hand to me? To God's representative?" Missionary Kwon ripped Bakjun's hands away from his shirt and pulled him up, dangling him in the air. "We're giving you an opportunity! And you can't stay still for five minutes to draw strength from his words when there's hundreds of thousands of your people who live on garbage every day!"

Cheolmin bit the missionary's hand and forced him to release Bakjun. Cheolmin said, "One! Two! Three!" and they tipped the missionary over as if he were a pine tree.

The missionary shouted, threatened. "Yongju! Yongju!" he pleaded. I didn't let anyone help him. Sweat rimmed his lips and the bridge of his nose, soaked his collar. His limbs jolted like an epileptic's. The boys were as excited as a pack of dogs, and their movements shook the lantern on the *saang*. Their hands had finally found an object for their anger and they kicked and punched and tore, communicated in a language they understood.

Their hands were my hands. Because I now knew hands blistered and feet cracked white by the weather. How to sleep with rats the size of rabbits, how to endure the slow crawl of lice. How drinking helped you live with unlivable fear. How you could wake up with frozen icicles in your hair, not knowing if one of the boys would be frozen dead, forever fourteen. How being locked in was a kind of daily death. I understood what it meant to be a North Korean in China. Because I was one of them.

Jangmi flew out from behind me and pried Bakjun's hands from the missionary's chest, but Cheolmin pushed her away and she fell. She limped in a fretful semicircle around them like a stray cat. She clutched her stomach, her phantom child.

I felt helpless. There was nothing I could do for her or for any of the people I had lost. When I closed my eyes, I saw Missionary Kwon's dirty hands on her body. The cycle was as clear to me as a simple sentence; I wanted to break it.

"Is this your plan? Simply to hurt him and release your anger, then wait for your punishment? Tie him up," I said. "Make him call a broker and get us out of this country. One of us can stay and watch him while the others leave—maybe Daehan?

"Or I'll stay." My thoughts spun beyond me.

I came back from the kitchen with the laundry cord and the kitchen scissors, and instructed the others to hold down his arms and legs. I sawed the rope into two with the scissors and used half to strap his arms so tightly back that the white shirt buttons strained against the convex curve of the missionary's stomach.

By the time Daehan returned, my work was done. When he saw us, his hands rammed into his crinkly hair and raised it into a bush. "Oh no, no!" he said. "You've got to stop!"

I didn't want it to stop.

"How dare you? Boys, calm down! Let's discuss this!" our overthrown ruler said. His muddled roil of thoughts were more a trail of panic than sentences. He pleaded, threatened. "Lord, why have you forsaken me?"

"Do something!" Daehan screamed at me, assuming it was the work of the others. He hurled himself at my back; I shook him off.

He said, "You're sabotaging yourself! I'm getting you help, I promise!" It sounded like another futile Christian promise.

"Watch this." Namil checked to see if we were watching,

then grabbed the scissors from me and slashed the window's covering, which was sticky with the cicadas, and wrapped it around Missionary Kwon's head.

The missionary shook his head wildly, trying to shake off the plastic. "It doesn't get better—your lives will feel like a dream and no one will ever understand you again once you cross. But I understand. God understands. You North Koreans are always so ungrateful."

The legs of his chair lifted and thudded against the floor as he struggled. The boys looked at one another for what to do next.

I withdrew one of the cell phones from Missionary Kwon's jacket pocket and scrolled through the list of names. "Which one leads us to a broker?"

The missionary sat up straight in the chair and his arms went limp in their binding. He took a deep breath, and panic and anger eased from his face until his glacial gaze went right through me.

"You think I care about this body, this mere shell?" he said. "You think that God is so weak, for you to threaten me?"

"All you have to do is get us out of here. You drove us to this."

"I saved you, all of you. Without me, you're nothing. Less than vermin."

Cheolmin spat on the floor near the missionary's feet. "What did you say?"

The missionary didn't stop there. He compared us to germs and parasites. Black spots danced in front of my eyes.

"If I made a phone call tomorrow, you'd disappear. Another call, you cross the Thailand border. I'm the one who decides.

Don't you see?" His mouth twisted upward into a mournful smile. "Who's going to know about you if I'm gone? Or care?"

My hands reached for the hard knob of his throat. The escaping air whistled from his pressurized pipe. No one, finally, was there for me. It wasn't Missionary Kwon facing me anymore but the darkness pursuing us. People crowded my eyes, voices knocked against one another. I was pushed back, backward, across the river. They were back, it was back.

I was surrounded by men, by hunting dogs. The ice gleamed silver moonlight as we crossed. The riverbed cut into my feet, and the mantraps lining the river opened and closed their mouths. There were traps everywhere, and mouths, and eyes. The eyes and mouths moved across us. I was there, we were there. I struck out at the Dear Leader, the red leather jacket, at the hands that pulled me down. Water surrounded us. We were drowning together.

Then I was dragged back from drowning. I gagged. The kitchen scissors were in Jangmi's hands and my hands were around hers. Our hands were dark and wet and smelled of fresh liver. Voices erupted. The missionary was on the floor and the boys were kicking him. The blood trickling from the missionary's eye glowed in the lantern's light. His gurgled screams filled the air; his shirt was a river of blood. That severed voice, those tattered ribbons of sound, were the only sounds he managed. As if his tongue was mourning his eye. I stared at his bruised arms and chest, his punctured eye socket. At my hands. They had held but not stopped Jangmi.

Daehan walked backward, leaving pale red tracks on the

cement floor. He held his stomach. "I want to go home," he whispered.

"*Meojori!*" Cheolmin looked impressed. "A *woman* did that?"

"Let him bleed to death." Bakjun's voice was small and unconvinced.

Namil gnawed at his fingernail, staring down at the missionary.

Gwangsu began to pray.

"Did I do that?" Jangmi's pupils were dilated.

From somewhere distant I heard Daehan say, "He needs help. He has a son." He wiped the blood from Missionary Kwon's face with the edge of his shirt. "Where's his phone? I'll call that doctor."

"You'll get us sent back!" Cheolmin punched Daehan in the stomach. "You're not calling anyone."

Jangmi clutched the bloody kitchen scissors to her shirt, shivering. Her hand ripped at her hair as if she were trying to wake herself up with pain.

Now we would never leave, I thought. "We need to call someone, anyone. We need to get out."

"Help is coming." Daehan made a sound between a sniffle and a moan. "Help was already coming. Give me the phone."

For forty-eight hours we waited in the thick of the missionary's mortified flesh that only Daehan approached and fed, as flies buzzed and laid their eggs in the submarine heat. We simmered in our fear until at the designated time we crossed the small stone bridge that led to a muddy country road, took several turns as instructed, and eventually, behind an abandoned village school, we met the brokers that Daehan's *eomeoni* had hired. I didn't know who Daehan was. It didn't matter anymore.

This is how it happened. We fled in the brokers' footsteps. We scattered into small dark spaces in the backs of buildings, trains, and buses, through the great mouth of China. Our feet made fresh tracks as we weaved through mountains and made unreliable allies of the moon and the night and the stars. Every shadow a soldier, a border guard, an opportunist. Each body of water reminded us of the first river, the river of dreams and death, where we saw the faces of people we knew and would never know frozen beneath it. The children who had run and been caught and sent back. The pregnant women repatriated to our country and thrown in jail, forced to run a hundred laps until they aborted. The women who gave birth in the same jail and saw soldiers bash their new infants against a wall to save bullets. The countless others whose peaceful lives ended when an enemy informed on them—ours was one small story in all the other stories. We stumbled across the jungles and deserts of Southeast Asia, seeking safety and freedom. We would look and look. A few of us would find it.

Part IV

Freedom

19

Danny

Maps are borders that keep people in and others out. My brand-new U.S. passport, which the immigration officer stamps for me at the Yanji airport, a modern surveillance tool. I made it past twenty and am several inches taller than my parents now; I'm half a semester away from a degree in sociology at Harvard, and only occasionally lapse back into supersonic leaps of speech. There are other changes, too. For example, it only takes me a few minutes in China to discover that my Chinese isn't what it used to be. In any case, after my digital fingerprints and photograph are taken for the first time, I step through the arrivals gate and into an old map, the topography of my past.

I look for my mom in the crowd of anxious faces. The airport echoes with the singsong seesaw of our Joseon language, which is so different from the rat-tat-tat of American English. I'm tired out from the flight, and the fluorescent blue chairs seem to beckon. The deacon spots me before I can dodge him and migrates through the curtain of noisy reunions, then stretches his hand my way as if we are in America. Next thing I know, he'll try to act like a father to me.

"You're all grown up, Daehan." He seems determined not to acknowledge our most recent encounter, when I found him six years ago curled up boomerang-style in my mom's wardrobe. "We're so glad you finally came."

I stay civil but I don't smile. That would feel like a betrayal of my dad, though from the way my old man reacted to the divorce, you would think that nothing has changed. He's still devoted to his time-pieces, still plays *baduk* weekly with the same two friends. Worst of all, he still lives alone, with only me to call him once a week to make sure he isn't surviving solely on microwave meals. The only times I know he is affected are when by necessity my mom's name comes up on my visits home and his eyes mist over as he polishes his spectacles.

"Call me shameless."

I hide my irritation even though my mom has broken promise number one: to leave the deacon at home. I've gotten better at forgiving.

"I'll go anywhere if someone else is paying for the plane ticket."

She comes up behind him in a hunter-green down coat and coordinating red scarf. A veritable Christmas tree, though my boyfriend would say that I don't fare much better in the fashion department.

"My Dumbo!" She looks elated and cautious all at once.

"Mom!"

We suffocate each other with hugs as if she hadn't just visited me in Boston four months ago, and in her arms I immediately feel more at home. She squeezes my cheeks with both hands. "I'm so, so happy you're here."

"Mom! I'm a little too old for public demonstrations."

"You're my *saekki*." Her smile is framed by crevices that seem to deepen by the month. "You're never too old."

She aims up to kiss me, but I dodge it by stretching to my fullest height.

"How was the flight?"

"The way it always is. Uncomfortable."

She tugs at my ear. "Did you read many books?"

I take her hands in mine and feel how dry and flaky they've become after the long Chinese winter. "I thought you were coming alone," I say, my voice lowered.

She pulls away. "I—I need the bathroom before we go." She dashes off, leaving me alone with the deacon.

I scoot my suitcase out of the way of passing travelers and plant myself on one of the plastic chairs. All of the airport's surfaces are coated in early spring's film of yellow dust. The deacon trails after me.

When he leans down to make eye contact, I fiddle with my luggage tags.

"You're not going to avoid me forever, are you? I'm part of your family now."

"I already have a family."

"Don't blame your *eomma*. She wanted me to stay at home." Home.

"I imagine you don't want to see me."

I finally look up. "You are responsible for my parents' divorce."

"I had to come out since you refused to see me. I wanted to . . . apologize."

I clap for him. "And now you've apologized."

"I'm a hypocrite, Daehan. I'm a sinner. We all are."

"I've figured out that much myself by now."

"This isn't easy for an adult to do—apologizing."

"What's your apology going to do—repair my parents' marriage? It doesn't change anything—it only makes you feel better."

He draws back as if I'd punched him. "Your *eomma* tells me you stopped going to church. It's my duty—my responsibility—to say this one thing: Don't rebel against your faith because you've lost faith in other people. I'm asking you, for the sake of your soul, don't confuse God with man."

Waves of fatigue wash over me. I think he's wrong about rebellion. Every day I mourn the loss of God, which also equaled the loss of my childhood. My faith was the greatest, most reassuring map of my life. But my doubts certainly aren't his business, so I say, not entirely untruthfully, "I've been on two flights for a total of over sixteen hours. I'm trying my very best to be civil."

I watch the rusty wheels of suitcases scrape past us and, in the silence, wait.

After saying our good-byes to the deacon, my mom and I drive through the smog and traffic that personify the new China, then along the border. She switches on an air freshener that smells of dried apples, and when she pulls off her sun hat before we leave the motel where we spent the night, the new sprays of gray hair shine in the sun. She notices me looking and says she'll dye it as soon as I leave for the States. Even her last name has changed.

As she drives now, she puckers her lips, soundlessly forming words and sentences the way she does when she's trying to find the right words. Finally she says, "I know you really wanted to go back to that house, but returning there doesn't seem such a good idea. Why not just visit the mountains and my hometown?"

"I need to face it."

Six years have passed, but in some ways time has stayed still for me. I know where I have to go.

"You're certain about this."

I nod, afraid my voice will crack if I say anything.

"A lot has changed, hasn't it?" She charges ahead. "There's a surplus of missionaries here now looking for Han people to convert. I've decided to return to California once the year's out, since I'm no longer needed here."

"With that man."

"Dumbo, he's my husband."

I tell her to veer right out of the city on the next road, which she does.

She says, "You're still not going to church."

"No, Mom."

"And you won't reconsider."

I give myself a moment to think. "It would be dishonest."

"So . . . when do I get to meet this girlfriend of yours? Maybe the next time I'm in America?"

"We've dated for less than two months. It's very present tense—it's not like we're getting married."

"Will you at least be on the same coast after you graduate? She sounds so nice . . ."

Meaning, she sounds like good wife material. I refrain from telling my mom that my girlfriend isn't exactly a girl. Or telling her that I don't know where I'll end up or what I want to become, or whether I'm made for a traditional wife-and-two-kids kind of life or something radically different. Leaving the church was bad enough and I don't have the courage yet.

"I haven't thought that far," I say. "You know I applied everywhere—law school, master's in sociology, management. Whoever gives me money."

"You still don't know what you want to do, do you?" Her fingers tighten around the wheel.

I shrug. "I'm okay with not knowing. It's not like you can perfectly navigate your way through life."

Everything is smaller at the border than I remembered it. The houses, the trees, the river itself. March isn't as cold as the March in my memory. The Tumen River is narrower. More puddles of water in the dry season than a river. The long stretch of border looks mainly peaceful despite the new surveillance cameras, where there weren't cameras before, and now much of the river is lined with barbed wire like cake icing and the new concrete holding centers that imprison North Koreans before they're sent back home to certain danger. In any case, it's hard to believe this river was the site of the claustrophobia, the fear, and the violence that the border has come to represent to me. We drive by the river-hugging small huts that my mom says are mainly owned by crooks trafficking North Korean women. The guard posts have now given way to camouflaged dugouts. The men still fish in the shallow water, a woman is doing laundry, and kids are skipping stones during what should be school hours.

I was there. I was a witness.

"But, Danny, you're okay, aren't you?"

Smugglers trundle their goods to one another across the river, using a rope and pulley system. She knows almost nothing about what happened to me in China no matter how she tries to wrangle it out of me; all she knows of that time is that I lived in a cave dugout with North Koreans, who later, in groups of twos or threes, were met at locations assigned to them at the last minute by human smugglers, arrangements she had made with great difficulty, jeopardizing her evangelical work with the Han Chinese. She knows that I'd witnessed the violence done to Missionary Kwon but didn't call for medical help until my friends were out of his reach.

I keep my eyes on the divided country across the river. "Mom, do you think the North and the South will ever be unified?"

"Your friends will meet their families again someday. If it's God's will."

"Was it God's will that they lived in a cave? Even in March, it gave a new definition to the word cold."

She looks guilty, pained. "I'm sorry, Daehan, I'm so sorry for everything."

I want to tell her it isn't her fault. To say that I'm now fairly confident that I'll live a fairly happy life, whatever that means. That I finally understand the impossibility of orchestrating the future or who I am. That I sometimes dream of rivers of floating eyes. That all of those eyes are Missionary Kwon's. Instead I massage her shoulder. "I've had a break," I say. "I can take over the driving now."

We finally arrive. I had assumed that images would come rushing back to me as soon as I faced the building, like in a movie, but nothing of the sort happens. Shredded, weather-worn Bubble Wrap hangs from the windows, the building's walls are streaked green with water stains, and the stairwell is rusted orange to the point of looking dangerous. In the building's shadows, the ice is still hard and stubborn.

My mom stays in the car as I walk toward the building. The yard's the same tangle of knee-high weeds. I think about the little I learned about my friends through my mom's contacts. Gwangsu out-Christianed the zealous South Korean church community, and after a couple of years in Daegu working odd jobs, he got a scholarship to seminary school. Namil was placed with adoptive parents through a Korean American church in Fairfax, Virginia. Bakjun ended up in Seoul, but after brawling in the kimchi factory he worked at whenever someone called him a spy or a dirty North Korean, he successfully applied a second time for refugee status in England, citing discrimination in the South, and settled in a New Malden boardinghouse. No one knows what happened to Cheolmin. Then there's Yongju. And Jangmi. I haven't heard from either of them since receiving a single phone call through the broker, letting me know they had reached safety. Halfway up the stairs, I stop. It's better not to continue.

As we drive back, my mom says, "Your friends, I hope they're doing well, wherever they are."

My eyes fill with the brown, bare landscape. "They're survivors," I say. This far north, it's as if winter never quite ended.

20

Yongju

At first there was loneliness. Then there was loss. And then there was a greater loneliness, the loneliness of freedom. Freedom: Once I am truly safe, I see that there is too much of it. Freedom means you are free not to care about anyone or anything. Freedom shows me that all that matters to the free world is money.

Before I understood what freedom meant, Jangmi and I blindly followed the broker through Chinese terrain ranging from bare plains to semitropical cities, then made that final jungle crossing from Laos into Thailand, where we sheltered each other for months in the crowded Bangkok detention center. The ground had shifted beneath me, becoming yet another new country, and the only stability was this primitive desire to live, and Jangmi. But in South Korea Jangmi and I were separated by a mosaic of men from their National Intelligence Service, who put me through weeks of lengthy security interrogations. Then I was finally admitted into the Hanawon resettlement center for the three months of required reeducation. I grieved, but I couldn't hold on to anger; it moved through my hands like water. I didn't feel trapped like the others, who were impatient to start a new life outside of the brick building's lecture rooms and routines; I was looking for Jangmi.

That first week I discovered her after a talk given by one of our people who had resettled in the South years ago.

The man at the podium had a face shiny with moisturizer and wore his collar flipped up like Elvis. He said, "I was you once," with the flat cadence of someone from Seoul, most of his Pyongan region accent rubbed out. He gave us warnings I didn't understand yet as he relayed his experience of resettling, and proudly mentioned having a South Korean wife. His exertions were wasted. I was in the back, and in front of me rows of heads hung heavily like a field of sunflowers.

I saw Jangmi in the corridor after I left the lecture room.

Though we all wore the same orange jacket and black pants, I recognized her from her feline movements and the drag of one foot. Her arms were linked with the arms of two other women heavier-set than she was, and I sprinted forward until I got ahead of them and confirmed that it was her. The same harmonious proportion of eyes to nose to lips, tension alive in her every gesture. She was laughing, her smile as bright as the cheap rhinestone pin in her hair. My family's background had slowed down my interrogation, and I later learned that she had been in Hanawon at least a month longer than me. It was as if she had moved so fast that the past couldn't catch up with her. She was already blooming in this new country.

"Jangmi!" I said.

All the light in her disappeared and her arms dropped limply to her sides. We had hidden, pressing together in filthy train bathrooms and clawing our way through suffocating jungles, trusting whatever the broker told us to do. She was the only person in the country who knew me. Her eyes clouded over and she swerved away from me as if I were a distant, unpleasant memory, uncoupling herself from her friends.

I grabbed her wrist. "Jangmi," I said again.

"You know I wouldn't go by that name anymore," she said. "It's old-fashioned, anyway."

A bright smile overwhelmed her again as if she was determined to cover up the past. I wanted to reach her, but I didn't know where to start, and the oppressive wall of her face seemed a kind of plea.

I said, "I just arrived. They kept me longer than I'd imagined, cross-referencing and checking and double-looping my words back to me, until I couldn't have lied even if I wanted to." Except about Missionary Kwon. Always about Missionary Kwon.

"I'm leaving here soon enough. I didn't have your kind of family," she said.

"Have you seen the others?"

"Why would I want to?" She cupped her hands together as if to share a secret and said, "You should keep your eyes and ears open here—there's a lot you can learn outside the classroom, if you pay attention."

I took her chin in one hand and made her look directly at me. "I know you. You don't have to pretend with me."

"You're always living in the past. I belong to the future, I always have." She stepped back. "It's dangerous to live in the past."

She turned away from me, and I understood that the ghost of Missionary Kwon was standing between us.

I knew how to wait. I knew how to be patient.

In South Korea, I meet a few of our people who have become brokers themselves and forge new routes out of China to bring our people to safety. I meet a South Korean Christian couple who sold their house and used that money to get people out. But I am no hero. I am one of the lucky ones. I studied for the college entrance exams and then matriculated into a famous university in Seoul. I work part-time for the South Korean government as a source of information on the North. I write for the university newspaper, hand out flyers about the human rights crisis in our country to impervious crowds, help release giant helium balloons with supplies and information north across the thirty-eighth parallel toward home. Home, a country that feels more like my country the longer I live in the South, which will never let us forget. I am a model North Korean refugee; I testify in front of churches, to the National Assembly, to anyone who will listen. I make endless inquiries into my family's fate, striking back in my small way at the gated mansion that took my *abeoji,* at the man in the red leather jacket. I have returned to China several times on my South Korean passport that has my new name, following tendrils of rumors about my *eomeoni,* my *dongsaeng.*

I haven't found them yet, though I did meet one woman who described my *dongsaeng* perfectly; the woman had been married off to a farmer, then fled the village during a crackdown. I did not give up. I tried dating strangers who remained strangers. And I did find the public housing apartment unit assigned to Jangmi. Two years passed before I dared write to her the first letter, then the second. A third. When she doesn't respond, I understand. Sometimes the memory is as much as you can bear.

On Saturday I enter the empty church and slide onto a darkly stained pew as I often do, and force myself to return to the border that haunts my sleep. I return to Missionary Kwon, his image burning into my sight. To the Dear Leader, crossing borders in a green Soviet train with its curtains lowered so that no one can see in or out. To signboards of blood-red Chinese characters. To boys living in a cave, so gaunt that their cheekbones strain out of their skin. To the gun aimed at my *abeoji*'s heart. To the last sight of the women in my life. I carry my other countries inside me.

As I wait for the bus back home to Kunsan, Seoul's Saturday night crowd is awakening. Teenagers dressed like American rap singers pass, the girls with the same reproduced narrow, tilted-up nose, flaunting skirts that are more slips of fabric than clothes, flash the logos once coveted by my *eomeoni*'s peers. A middle-aged woman waits in a ruffled miniskirt, as if she couldn't bear parting with an image of her twenty-year-old self. The café in front of the stop is lined with books, its ceiling as high as a church steeple. You could buy a kilo of rice back home for the price of an Americano. I am often bitter; I am always nostalgic.

I find Jangmi's letter in my neglected mailbox. The plain white envelope is the sort sold in twenty-four-hour convenience

Krys Lee

stores, and my address, a smudge of blue ink, as if she half-hoped that I would not receive it.

In the apartment nearly as empty of possessions as the day I moved in, I wait as long as I can bear. I open the window and let in the early spring air, face its chilly fingers and try to stay calm. It might be a cursory note directing me to never write to her again. A colorful declaration of disgust at my epistolary rituals. She might mock my certainty that she is the only woman who can ever really know me, brand me as a man stuck reading the past. Which I am. My hands shake as I cajole the envelope open, careful not to rip it.

21

Jangmi

The letter is sent, and it's too late to take it back. I realize what this means as I sink into the largest tub in the bathhouse. I press against a shooting jet of water, its force compounding the pounding of my heart. The bubbling water swells up my nose. I proposed the meeting in a weak moment, but I don't have to show up. I can leave Yongju alone waiting on the beach in front of the Paradise Hotel to watch the sunrise by himself.

It won't be a completely wasted trip to Pusan for him; there is the fish market, the beach boardwalk. The Pusan film festival exhibition hall to visit. I stay in the steaming water and watch the naked bodies of women surrounding me. They are dragged down by hanging breasts and wide thighs wrinkled like tissue paper. Weary bodies, my *eomma*'s body, the kind of body that will someday be mine. I decide I will arrange another phone call to her that week, no matter what it costs to pay the broker. For there is a broker for everything north and south of the thirty-eighth parallel. A thriving industry has grown up around us.

I plunge into the cold pool then back to the hot, going from scalding to frozen, trying to distract myself. As I cross back to the cold pool, a *halmeoni* with thready gray hair and a bulbous stomach pinches my butt cheek as if my body is hers and says, "If you young ones had gone through the postwar years you wouldn't be skimping! You'd know the value of food."

I have known all kinds of hunger, but I am tired of fighting. In my best standardized South Korean accent I just say, "Halmeoni, you must have had a hard life."

In the steaming room I listen patiently as she begins sharing the stories she must have needed to tell.

I once saw a person swept under the Tumen River's summer currents. I got a single look at him before the square-jawed man sank into the swollen river. It happened years ago, but in Pusan his body returns to me in dreams. I see his hands reaching for anything to hold on to and his fingernails catching and tearing on an azalea bush. His brown face bobs up, down, and his wide-open mouth floods with water. His body floats downstream until his foot lodges between two rocks and his limbs fan out like kelp. Only then do I turn his body over and see Missionary Kwon.

The day I'm to meet Yongju, I wake up early. The missionary's sightless eye hovers outside the window where the moon should be. My breath draws sharply in. It's just an image, I tell myself. An image that sometimes compels me to church. The past, my unborn infant, is always with me. I force myself to get up. The common room is weighed down with objects as if I have lived there for decades. Nothing useful escapes me: bundles of old cooking magazines, tossed-out construction gloves, abandoned bookshelves and chairs, orphaned buttons and safety pins, a straw basket choking with coupons. Between full-time work as a receptionist and night school, I rip through charity shops, looking for bargains that don't look like bargains. My apartment empty of people, the way I wanted it.

It is possible to live happily forever alone. That is what I told myself. Still, I take care before I leave the apartment early in the morning, applying makeup, curling my hair. I pass stores with their metal shutters pulled down and wait for the bus toward Haeundae Beach. I whirl around at footsteps behind me, but there is no one there.

The only people out near Haeundae are drunk, sleeping men, couples, and a few hostess-room girls returning home in tight black dresses and fur coats. I blush just looking at them, but their smoky eye shadow makes me wonder if the blue I usually apply marks me as old-fashioned or worse, from the North, like my accent that reappears in traces and words from home that sometimes tumble from my lips. There is my bad leg that has never quite healed, which drags a beat behind the rest of me.

The shore is as grainy as sandpaper on my bare feet, but it feels good to walk. Here I am, living in a port city, and six months have passed since I visited the beach. A wave hits the shore, then a larger one collides into it and swallows it up. I wade knee-deep in the freezing water, my bare feet clammy with salt and sand. My cardigan ripples around me; my hair tangles in the salty air. I feel lighter than I have in years. I wonder if I will reach another reality if I keep walking.

Then I spot Yongju staring down at a crowd of hermit crabs scrambling near his feet. He hasn't seen me yet, but it is as if he has touched me and awakened my sleepwalking body. He is wearing rumpled slacks, a white dress shirt, and a black wool coat as if for an interview, his silky hair blowing into his face. Though he has filled out from boy to man, a permanent storm of worry still creases his forehead. I see the gaps in him as plainly as missing front teeth. He has known and experienced too much, but still I want to walk, to run to him, toward my real life.

I take a step back.

"Nuna," he says, looking up, the vowels in "Older Sister" made long and sinuous by his slow speech. "Jangmi."

I want to run away as fast as my bad leg will let me, preserve the peace I've worked so hard to build. Looking at him, my old fears flare up. My heart comes alive. Yongju is complication, a wound ripped open. He's a student, a North Korean with little to offer. I know there are no happy endings. But I don't run. This time I stay.

Acknowledgments

I am grateful to Kathryn Court, Lindsey Schwoeri, and everyone else at Viking Penguin for making this a better book, and to my agent, Susan Golomb, who has been my sound guide.

Many friends read and commented on the novel at different stages: Rachel Howard, Kim Stoker, Joanna Hosaniak, Lillian Lee, and Anthony Adler. Jean Lee and others who prefer to remain anonymous gave valuable advice. Doosung Lee gave me a lovely place to write when I needed it most. My students Dongrim Song, Wontaek Lee, Sangyeop Lee, Seokjin Yun, Joon Oh, and Hani Lee helped me along the way.

To Dong-hyuk Shin, survivor and brave friend. I owe Amy Lee and Kye Myeong Lee all my gratitude and love. To all the great, brave women in my life—I wouldn't have made it all the way here without you.

The nonprofit organizations Citizens' Alliance for North Korean Human Rights and Justice for North Korea do inspiring work devoted to the safety and resettlement of North Koreans

Acknowledgments

fleeing their country, and also created international awareness about the human rights crisis at a time when few knew or cared.

For their generous support, I am indebted to the Toji Cultural Center, the American Academy in Rome, and the American Academy of Arts and Letters.